WHERE IS THE LOVE

MONICA WALTERS

INTRODUCTION

Hello, readers!

Thank you for purchasing and/or downloading this book. This work of art contains explicit language, lewd sex scenes, moments of depression/grief, and topics that may be sensitive to some readers.

This is book sixteen of an existing series of books, The Henderson Family Saga. If you have not read them, you will not understand a thing. Character development happened in previous books of the family series. It's *highly* recommended that you read the previous books of this family's series before indulging in this one, because it updates family dynamics that I don't go into great detail about.

Blindsided by Love
Ignite My Soul
Come and Get Me
In Way Too Deep
You Belong to Me
Found Love in a Rider

INTRODUCTION

Damaged Intentions: The Soul of a Thug
Let Me Ride
Better the Second Time Around
I Wish I Could Be the One
I Wish I Could Be the One 2
Put That on Everything: A Henderson Family Novella
What's It Gonna Be?
Someone Like You
A Country Hood Christmas with The Hendersons

Also, please remember that your reality isn't everyone's reality. What may seem unrealistic or unrelatable to you could be very real and relatable to someone else. But also keep in mind that despite the previous statement, this is a fictional story.

Jessica had quite a few options, but I hope you enjoy the ride her story will take you on. Enjoy!

Monica

Henderson Family and Friends Family Chart
Wesley and Joan Henderson (Patriarch and Matriarch)

Wesley Jr. (Olivia)
Nesha (WJ's daughter w/ Evette)
Shakayla and Chenetra
(WJ's daughters w/ ex-wife, Sharon)
Decaurey (Olivia's son)

Jenahra (Carter)
Jessica and Jacob (Joseph's kids)
Carter Jr. (CJ)

Chrissy (LaKeith)
Jakari, Christian, Rylan
(Avery's sons)
Janessa and LaKeith Jr. (LJ)
(LaKeith's kids w/ Nancy)

Kenny (Keisha)
Kendrall Jr.
Karima
Kendrick (Kenny's deceased son)
King
Kane

Jasper (Chasity)
Ashanni
Royal
Crew

Tiffany (Ryder)
Milana
Ryder Jr. (Ryder J or RJ)

Storm (Aspen)
Bali and Noni (twins)
Maui
Seven Jr. (SS)
Remington (Remy)

Marcus (Wesley's son) (Synthia)
Ace (Marcus's son w/ Heaven)
Malia (Marcus's daughter w/Mali)
Seneda (daughter w/ Syn)

Malachi (Danica)
(cousin of the Hendersons)
Malachi Jr. (MJ)
Deshon
Niara

Kema and Philly
(Tiffany's friend and Ryder's brother)
Philly Jr. and Philema (twins)
Kiana

Shylou and Cass
(Friends of Kenny and Keisha)
Shaydon
Shymir

Vida and Aston
Synthia (Marcus's wife)
(Vida's daughter with Jerome)

Nesha (WJ's daughter) & Lennox
Pregnant

Jessica (Jenahra's daughter)

Decaurey (WJ's stepson)

Jakari (Chrissy's son)

PROLOGUE
JESSICA

"I don't know what the fuck is going on with you, Decklan, but I'm tired of sticking around to be ignored and taken for granted."

"Baby, please don't do this. Jessica, I need you."

"Need me? You have a fucked-up way of showing that shit. For the past four months or so, you've been someone else. After Nesha and Lennox's wedding, I won't ever have to see you again. Although Lennox is your brother, I promise to miss as many family events as I can to avoid your ass. Just to think, I thought you would be the one for me. I'm not for the bullshit, but yet I've been dealing with the shit because I was falling for the man you showed me you could be. You left me emotionally, and the pussy you been dipping in, apparently, has all your attention."

I walked away from him and zipped my suitcase. After Christmas, I would be flying to New York for a photo shoot for a Nordstrom ad. When Decklan grabbed my arm to turn me back to him, I obliged him but slapped the shit out of his ass. My feelings were hurt as fuck. He didn't deny fucking around on me. I didn't have solid proof, because I wasn't a 'go through his shit' type of chick. I should be able to trust who I was with. However, the signs were there in his behavior.

The distance, decreased affection and attention, and the minimal communication were all signs that someone else was getting what I used to get from him. I didn't understand what had happened. Maybe I was working too much and not around enough. *Stop that shit, Jessica!* I refused to accept blame for his fuck ups. He knew what it was when he got involved with me.

He released me, and his hand went to his face as he frowned. It wasn't a frown of anger though. It was one of sorrow and remorse. The sight of it pulled the emotions out of me. The tears fell from my eyes, no matter how hard I was trying to hold them in. It had been a while since I had been hurt like this. After my last boyfriend and after Uncle WJ had handled my abusive father, I hadn't given having a man in my life a second thought.

That wasn't to say I didn't engage in ho activities from time to time, because I definitely did. Jasmine Sullivan had written that album *Heaux Tales* just for me. I was a single woman and could do what the fuck I wanted to do. Jessica Monroe could be a whole ass problem at times. I had niggas hunting me down to get that good good, and I would straight up ghost their asses afterward. Being plus sized didn't stop a nigga from fucking me or eating my pussy and the groceries. This sized eighteen frame didn't go unnoticed by anybody. I supposed I inherited my body type from Aunt Chrissy, along with the wagon I was dragging... my ass. My mama was slender and had been all her life.

After I got established in my career with my stepdad, Carter Wothyla and family friend, Shylou Smith, being a full-figured model, I wanted love... I was ready for it, especially after I saw how happy Nesha was with Lennox. When she told me he had a brother, I was all for the meet up.

For nearly an entire year, I'd been wined and dined by him. I could admit that I was a slow mover when it came to my emotions. I didn't want to reveal how I felt about a person too early, for fear of getting hurt... like I was now. It seemed he was the same way, because other than saying how attracted he was to me and how he needed me, the love word hadn't left his lips either.

I fell to my bed next to my suitcase and cried my eyes out for the first time in a while. I tried to be strong and not show weakness, but leaving Decklan had me so damn fragile. My heart was broken. *I love him.* I was glad I hadn't told him my true feelings, or he would be trying to play on them right now. It seemed he knew anyway, though, because he dropped his head to his hands for a moment, then lifted it and pulled me in his arms.

"I'm so sorry, Jess. Seeing you cry like this is heartbreaking, especially to know I'm the cause of it. Damn, baby. I don't know what got into me. I haven't been myself for the last few months, and I apologize sincerely for it. You mean so much to me, and I treated you like you didn't matter in my world. You right. I fucked up bad."

He kissed my head as I lay against him for what would be the last time. I was trying to wrap my mind around that and pull myself together. Life went on, and, unfortunately, it would be going on without him.

I WAS FUCKED ALL the way up. Although Nesha had said she didn't want to turn up before the wedding, her stepbrother, Decaurey, had told us he was taking us out to a trail ride and wasn't accepting no for an answer. It was actually the party after the trail ride. The actual ride had taken place earlier in the day. I'd been dancing with this fine ass country hood nigga almost all night. His hands had graced my curves, and his erection had been pressed against my ass all night as well.

After making my way back to the dance floor with my water, I noticed people crowding an area. I rolled my eyes. If these muthafuckas were fighting, I was gonna be so upset. I was having a great time and hadn't thought about Decklan once since I'd been dancing.

When a path started to clear out, I saw my cousins Jakari and Malachi. Right behind them was Nate... Nate fucking Guillory.

He was a professional basketball player, and he was one of Lennox's friends. That man was fine as hell, and I was about to lose the good sense God gave me just to get a taste. I'd just met him today at the wedding rehearsal, but I could barely take my eyes off him. We talked a bit and exchanged numbers. He'd texted me a couple of hours ago when we first got here, asking me to hit him up when I got settled for the night. Apparently, he couldn't wait until then.

The guy I'd been dancing with was right behind me, dancing on me as Nate approached. I hadn't stopped dancing, but our eyes were trained on each other's. When he stood his tall ass in front of me, I forgot all about the nigga behind me and walked away with him as he gave country hood a head nod. He grabbed my hand and brought it to his thick ass lips and kissed it. "When I heard your cousins say they were coming to meet y'all, I knew I had to come too. I've never been to a trail ride, and this seems pretty cool, but there was also a fine ass woman that I needed to see."

I had to be blushing hard as hell, because it felt like the temperature increased by twenty degrees. I didn't respond verbally. I just started grinding against him. With as tall as he was, it felt like I was only grinding against his leg. He gave me a slight smile, then said, "Why you didn't tell me you were involved with someone?"

I took a deep breath and tried to walk away, but he pulled me closer to him by wrapping his arm around me. He smelled so damn good. I slid my arms around his waist and laid my head on his chest for a few seconds. I was feeling so damn vulnerable. Nate didn't say anything else. He wrapped his arms around me and started to sway side to side. Thankfully, the DJ had started playing "Too Long" by King George, which was a mid-tempo cut.

When I pulled away from him, I didn't know what he saw in my eyes, but he leaned over and kissed my lips. I knew I had to be the envy of every woman in the place. I knew our attraction was so strong because I was vulnerable. From our talk earlier, I knew that he was looking for love. He was so sweet and caring. He was still leaned over, so I said in his ear, "We broke up a few days ago. We aren't involved anymore."

He stood up straight and stared into my eyes then brought his hand to my cheek. "He fucked over a good woman. He admitted that tonight in front of your cousins. I think that's another reason why they wanted to come out here instead of staying with him and Lennox. Although I don't really know your family, I asked to come because I needed to see about you and your heart."

Shit! Decklan was running his mouth big time. I did my best to make dealing with shit easy. No one knew how much I was really hurting. Nesha had a clue, which was why she was staring at us so hard. I was the hard one that always kept it together. Every issue I'd had in my life, I gave off the impression I didn't give a fuck. Deep down inside, I was just like Jenahra Henderson, before and after Joseph Monroe. I was strong, but I was weaker than I let on at times.

I dealt with insecurities, especially about my size and looks. Growing up, I never really saw myself as being beautiful, but instead of wallowing in that, I would make jokes about how beautiful I was. I eventually grew out of that and changed my mindset, but when Carter suggested that I work as a model for his boutique and for Shylou's clothing line, my confidence really went through the roof.

But here Nate was, after only being acquainted with me for a few hours, seeing what it took other people, even some of my family, months to see… if they ever saw it. I closed my eyes, willing myself not to cry. Nate gently caressed my cheek then pulled me into his embrace and started swaying again. Once the song went off, I lifted my head to see him talking to Jakari. When he noticed I was looking at him, he smiled. "You wanna get out of here?"

I only nodded. He licked his lips, grabbed me by the hand, and led me off the dance floor. Nesha gave me a pointed glare as I headed her way to tell her I was leaving. She kissed my cheek. "I hope you know what you're doing, Jess. You're vulnerable and drunk. That's not a good combination when you're around a sexy ass man that you barely know."

She was right, but I wasn't in the same mood I was in earlier. I wanted to fuck the dance floor up, give a nigga hope that didn't have a chance. Now I wanted to be loved on. I was so damn emotional, and Nate seemed to be sensitive to that. "Nesha, I'm a big girl. I can handle whatever comes of this. I handle things y'all don't have a clue about because I make that shit look easy. I got it."

Danica stared on, and I could see her huff slightly. "Jess, we're just worried about you. That's all," she said as Nesha nodded.

"Again, you don't have to worry. Jessica takes care of Jessica, and she's been doing a damn good job all by herself."

I walked away from them and met Nate over by Jakari. He'd given him his keys, so I assumed he and Mal were going to ride back with Decaurey. Jakari pulled me to him and said, "I believe you're in good hands, baby, but be careful. You know I got your back, always."

He kissed my cheek as I smiled up at him. I knew that if I ever needed them, my family wouldn't hesitate to have my back, especially Uncle Storm, Aunt Tiff, and Uncle Jasper. They were my protectors growing up since they were still kids when I was born. Uncle Storm and I were the closest since our personalities were similar. I wasn't nearly as rowdy as he was, but I could be if I needed to be.

Nate grabbed my hand, pulling me to him and wrapping his arm around me as we walked to Jakari's car. People were stopping him left and right, for pictures and autographs. One woman pulled her shirt down for him to sign her titty. He glanced at me, and I shrugged my shoulders. He wasn't mine, so I didn't care. He would be mine for tonight as soon as we left from here though.

When we got to Jakari's car, he opened the door for me and watched me get in... rather fall in. I chuckled to myself as he stood there with a serious expression on his face. "You good?"

"Yeah, I'm okay."

He closed the door and walked around to the driver's side. When he got in, he said, "A'ight. You gon' have to help me out of the sticks back to civilization. I know Beaumont since I grew up in H-Town. I have family there, so we visited often, but this area? A nigga is lost as hell."

I chuckled again. "I'm lit. I don't know how much help I'll be. I live in Houston and have been for twelve years or so."

"So you're saying we may have to thug it out in the woods?"

I laughed loudly, probably harder than I should have. It wasn't that funny, but he caught me off guard, and I was drunk. Nate chuckled along with me as I pointed in the direction he should go. When we got to Major Drive in Beaumont, he was good from there to find his hotel room at the Eleganté. My body heated up as he parked, and my nerves started overpowering my drunken state. He noticed because he grabbed my hand and said, "We ain't doing shit you don't want to do. Okay?"

I nodded, and he stroked my cheek then got out of the car to come open my door. My nerves dissipated for the moment. After he helped me out, I noticed my drunken state had gotten worse. I could barely walk. Without hesitancy, Nate picked my big ass up and held me in his arms like a baby. I couldn't help but stare into his eyes as he walked inside the hotel. *Damn, this man is so fine.*

The cameras were out, and pictures were being taken as he made his way to the elevator. I didn't even give a damn. I loosely circled my arms around his neck and rested my head on his shoulder. After getting inside the elevator, he lowered me to my feet and held me close to him. "Thank you, Nate. I really appreciate that. I know I'm heavy."

"You ain't heavy to a nigga like me. Don't mention it. I got'chu, and other than your beauty, I don't have a clue why. Something about you makes me wanna rescue you from the pain I see in your eyes. I don't even know who Jessica Monroe is, but I wanna be the one to make you happy."

I looked away from him and focused on keeping my balance. I couldn't respond to shit he said. His words were beautiful, but with as emotional as I was feeling, I'd be in a relationship with his ass before I left. Once the elevator doors opened, he grabbed my hand and led me to his suite. When he opened the door, I was in awe of how nice it was. I never knew the Eleganté had suites like this. Not paying attention to where I was walking, I nearly fell down the steps.

Nate caught me by my hips and steadied me then led me to the couch. "You okay?"

"Yeah. Thanks."

He sat next to me, and before he could say another word, I pulled his face to mine and kissed him, sliding my tongue to his, initiating the type of kiss I wanted from him. His hands slid around me, and he gripped my ass. I took further initiative and straddled him. He bit his bottom lip as he stared at me then brought his hands back to my ass. He grinded me on his dick, and my eyes rolled to the back of my head. I wanted him so bad.

His hands slid under my shirt, and he rubbed my back as he pulled away from me. He sat there just staring at me, like he was waiting to see what I would do next. I pulled my shirt over my head and unfastened my bra, causing him to sit up and immediately pull my nipple into his mouth. I grabbed at his shirt and pulled it over his head, forcing him to pause the way he was taking me to ecstasy, simply from sucking my nipple.

I stood from his lap and pulled at my leggings to get them down my legs as he unfastened his jeans and did the same. When I was done, he was sitting there in all his naked glory. "Damn, you fine. Six feet, ten inches of perfection and another damn foot hanging between your legs."

My mouth was watering, and I knew I had to taste him. I went to my knees in front of him and pulled the head of his dick between my lips. I began by sucking the head then swirling my tongue around it. "Ooooh, fuck! That feels good, Jessica."

His words fueled my fire, and I began taking more of him, watching the saliva travel down the rest of his dick to his balls. After a couple of minutes, he pulled me from it and stood from his seat. He helped me from the floor and took me to the bed. I sat and was about to scoot back until he knelt on the floor in front of me. I grabbed my ankles and lay back, giving him the showstopping view he wanted.

"Oh shit. She beautiful as fuck," he whispered before licking me from my entry to my clit.

My body shivered, and my eyes rolled to the back of my head as he made love to my pussy with his tongue. However, when my eyes rolled, all I saw was Decklan's pathetic ass. *Why is he on my mind now?* I swallowed hard and tried to concentrate on how Nate was making me feel. When he sucked my clit, I orgasmed, but it wasn't as intense as it normally was. I knew that was because my mind was fucked up.

Nate slid his fingers inside of me, and shit if that didn't feel good. I pulled his fingers from me and sucked them clean as he watched me. It looked like he stopped breathing. He glanced back down at my pussy, then put his entire face in it, bringing me to orgasm all over again. That time, it was intense as hell. I squirted everywhere as I screamed.

"Got damn, Jessica. That shit was sexy as fuck, baby."

I licked my lips and swallowed hard as he slid his fingers through my mess and brought them to his mouth to taste. He closed his eyes and moaned. "This some good shit. Where you been hiding at?"

Once again, Decklan entered my mind. He'd asked me the exact same question our first time having sex. I lowered my legs as Nate stood. He'd gone to his luggage, I assumed to look for a condom. The tears were falling down my face uncontrollably. Where was the love I was supposed to receive from Decklan? Why couldn't he do all the things he promised me he would do?

When Nate turned back to me and saw the tears on my face, he dropped the condom to the floor and joined me in bed. "I'm so sorry. I can't do this. I can't..."

"Shh. I can't say that I'm not disappointed, but it's okay. I understand. Just get some rest, and I'll take you home when I get Jakari's car back to him."

"You don't have to take me home. I can just drive it back."

"Naw. You drunk. I got'chu, baby. Just relax."

I lay in his arms and let him comfort me about a love lost. This shit was so unfair to him. After ten minutes, I got up and got dressed. Decklan had my mental so fucked up, I was about to fuck a damn stranger. This wasn't like me, and I refused to let what he put me through change me for the worse. It was time to be the strong woman I'd always been and bury that shit. *Fuck him.*

CHAPTER ONE

JESSICA

Three months later...

I'd just gotten to town to spend a week with my family for spring break. I was tired as hell. Although the drive was only about an hour and a few minutes from my apartment, I'd only gotten about three hours of sleep. I'd just gotten in from a shoot in Hawaii for *Sports Illustrated*. There wasn't a bitch alive who could tell me shit as I strutted my ass through that sand, posing for photos. I was paying for that shit today.

In fact, I was so damn tired I thought I saw a sign at Jasper's Liquor that Uncle Storm was running for mayor. The further I drove into town, the more of them I saw. I found myself laughing hysterically while I was driving. There was no way these white folks were going to vote his ass in office. I could see him now, acting like Councilman Mayes on TikTok. Secondly, it wasn't even election time.

However, it was the last couple of signs before getting to my parents' house that had my ass making a U-turn right in the middle of Highway 90 to go back to his house. That shit said, *I chase all sorts of*

Storms, including shit storms, because I'm the Storm chaser. They all have to bow to me. Then the second one said, It's only right to elect the watcher over the city. The Gabriel of Big City Nome, Texas, Storm 'Gabriel' Henderson. Then it had a picture of his ass with a halo over his head. This shit had to be a joke. I could barely drive from laughing so hard.

When I turned in his driveway, he was coming out of the backyard with a frown on his face and his phone in front of him. I did my best to contain my laughter as I got out of the car and heard him saying, "I'm gon' fuck somebody up. Although all that shit is true, they put them out at the wrong time. This shit got Jasper, Marcus, and Tiffany's names all over it."

He looked up at me and winked, then said, "Yo' daughter at my house. She came to see me before she went to see you. How you feel about that?"

"Jessica! Really?" my mom yelled from the phone.

I chuckled. "Mama, I'm sorry, but those signs distracted me. I made a U-turn in the middle of the highway."

She fell out laughing as Uncle Storm laughed sarcastically. "Bye, Jen."

He ended the call in her face and hugged me. "What's up, Ace?"

I chuckled. He used to call me his ace boon koon all the time when I was little, because I could be as rowdy as he was when Joseph wasn't around. Since Uncle Marcus had been a part of the family, he stopped calling me that. Uncle Marcus had a son named Ace. We had too many family members, so we had to keep these names straight. It was bad enough with Decaurey and Jakari. Their names were so damn close. It was easy to get them confused. Our saving grace was that Decaurey wasn't born in the family.

"Ain't nothing, Unc. Just worked the shit out of this shoot in Hawaii. You know how us Hendersons do it."

"Hell yeah. That's good. I'm proud of you. That nigga still tryna get back?"

"Yeah, but not aggressively. So you don't have to worry about anything like that. He just calls once a week to check on me and tells me he loves me," I said softly.

It was crazy that he even said that shit to me. He waited until we were no longer together to tell me he loved me. Who did shit like that? Of course, I didn't want to believe that it was sincere… that he was just trying to manipulate me into giving him another chance. My heart knew better though. The Decklan I knew and had fallen in love with didn't say shit he didn't mean. I just wished he wouldn't have told me. I kept my feelings to myself, and I refused to say it back to him.

"You never told me y'all were in love, Jess."

"We never said it to each other. I still love him, and it's been hard moving on, but I refuse to hang on to a man that can hurt me the way he did, Unc."

"Muthafucka needs his ass whupped. The only reason he hasn't gotten it already is simply because of Lennox. If he starts bothering you, let me know. You know we don't have a problem rolling out for our sisters and nieces."

"I know, Unc. I had to come by, though, and fuck wit'chu about those signs."

I laughed as he frowned again. "Uh huh. I'm about to go find Jasper's ass and fuck him up. I know he was behind that shit. I'm gon' pull all that shit up and use it when I run."

"You for real about that?"

"Hell yeah. Big City Nome need to make a comeback, and it starts with leadership. Muthafuckas around here ain't doing shit and don't know how to get funds out here to fix shit. Look how long it took the county to fix 3rd Street. That shit was ridiculous. Grayburg needs to be fixed too. All that patching they doing ain't doing shit but making it worse."

"You right. Let me get to Mama's house though. Are y'all still cooking at the barn this weekend?"

"Yep. We turning up Henderson style. Everybody supposed to fall through, even Legend and his basketball team."

"Unc, you can't talk. You have five kids too."

"I know, but mine further apart in years. The twins are sixteen, and Remy is barely four. Legend's are all back to back, so they can all play on the same team."

I rolled my eyes. "On that note, I'm out."

"A'ight. See you later."

I got in my car to head home but saw my mama turning in the diner parking lot. She'd told me that they extended their hours on Thursdays to have a family night. They stayed open until eight. I glanced at my phone to see it was only five. I turned in the parking lot to go in and say hi to Aunt Chrissy. I noticed her car was there.

When I walked in, there was so much laughter it caused me to smile. I walked in the kitchen to see Aunt Chrissy and Aunt Tiffany nearly doubled over from laughing so much. Uncle Jasper said, "That nigga gon' be coming for me in a minute, so y'all better have my back. I didn't make those signs by myself."

I joined in with the laughter, and they all turned to me. My mama ran to me like she hadn't seen me in years. We talked almost every day. Since my breakup with Decklan, we'd been talking more. I had a real problem with talking to her about relationship drama. Watching her endure abuse from Joseph for over twenty years made me somewhat dislike her. I loved her as my mother, but her allowing that man to demean her and me, bothered me. He was the reason I had issues with the way I looked.

'Til this day, although he's been dead for six years, his hateful words came to my mind, and I sometimes had nightmares about him. He was also the reason I had a problem trusting people. He was my father, despite my ability to refer to him as such. He was the man that should have loved me the most. When Uncle WJ killed him, I felt a sense of relief. It was like my mother was in bondage as long as he was alive. She was free to live her life on her terms, and that freed me. I never went to that house to visit after I moved out.

I refused to visit him, especially since he was still treating my mother like his slave. I threatened to tell my uncles several times, but my mother told me she would never forgive me if I did. She taught me to endure bullshit. That was something I had to rid myself of. It wasn't hard to do that, though, because it was never something I wanted to do.

After hugging and kissing everyone, the smell of the food had my stomach growling loud as hell. I went to the steam tables up front to fix myself a plate, only to see they had a customer waiting. Just as I was about to call one of them up front, he said, "Jess?"

I stared up at him with a slight frown, then suddenly, realization of who he was came to me. "Brix?"

He smiled, and his eyes narrowed to slits as they always did. I ran around the steam table and gave him the biggest hug. We went to school together, from kindergarten to twelfth grade, and took plenty of classes together. We were good friends until we entered the dating phase. It was like the people we dated thought we had a thing for each other when we were truly just friends. He picked me up and swung me around, causing me to squeal. He always did that shit.

I laughed as he put me down. "My God! How have you been? It's been like twelve or thirteen years since I've seen you! You never came home to visit?"

He chuckled. "Yeah. I've come home. It just seemed we always missed each other. What you been up to? You looking good," he said as he scanned my body.

My nipples hardened a bit, and I was confused about that. Although I had been slightly attracted to Brixton, we were friends. He was a nice-looking guy. We just never went there. Now, he was an even better-looking man. He looked like he lived in the gym. His muscles were visible every-damn-where.

"Thank you. I'm modeling now. Best decision I've ever made. Besides living in the gym, what are you doing?"

He chuckled and gave me an under-eyed look that he used to give to girls in school all the time. "I'm a personal trainer, and I own a gym in Austin. So I guess I don't do anything besides live in the gym."

"Well, what brings you back?"

"My dad died a few months back, and my grandparents' land has just been sitting there going to shit since he was an only child. I decided to come home to work it and get it back up to par. I mean, it ain't on the level of the Hendersons and all, but it made him a little money."

"There you go, being a hater. How's your sister?"

"She's good. She lives in New York."

"Damn. She stayed there after college, huh?"

"Yeah. She loved it."

"Okay, so what do you want to eat?"

"Stuffed chicken. They've done a great job expanding the place. It looks really good."

"Yeah. They expanded a couple of years ago."

He nodded as I fixed his plate. I could feel him staring at me, and that shit had me antsy. Brix was a forward guy in school. I wondered if he was still that way. I could see him watching my every move like he was memorizing my features and mannerisms. I looked up at him and said, "Go ahead and get you something to drink."

He smiled and nodded as I added beans and greens to his plate. I fixed myself a plate, then took them both to the table. Chrissy and Mama could complain about him getting a free meal all they wanted to. They should have had their asses on their jobs. When he returned, he set a glass of Fanta orange in front of me. I smiled hard as hell and immediately took a sip of it. "Thank you."

"Thank you for fixing my food. You ain't finna get me in trouble for not paying though. You know yo' mama don't play about her money."

I chuckled. "She doesn't, but they are too busy back there laughing about Uncle Storm and forgetting that they have a business to run."

"What's he up to? Is he still mean?"

WHERE IS THE LOVE

"Hell yeah. That's just Uncle Storm. He's lightened up a little over the years, but he's still crazy as hell."

Brix nodded and reached for my hands. I smiled slightly and put them in his so he could bless our food. I glanced at him to see he'd closed his eyes. I chose to keep mine open so I could look him over the way he'd done me. God had done a work on his ass. He was somewhat on the thin side in school and had a clean face. He still had a young-looking face, but that beard said he was a grown ass man.

When he finished the prayer, I smiled at him and was about to dig into my red beans and rice when I heard, "Where his ass at?"

I rolled my eyes as Brix looked toward the kitchen. When Uncle Jasper came running through the diner with Uncle Storm right behind him, the entire area erupted in laughter. Everybody knew those fools liked to cut up. My mama and Aunt Chrissy came from the back. "So sorry, everybody, for our brothers' childish behavior. They mean no harm. If you saw all the mayor signs all over town, that's what this is about," my mama said, barely able to contain her laughter.

She glanced over at me then Brix, and her eyes widened. She knew about our friendship in school, but it was something we had to keep between us, or Joseph would have put a stop to it. She made her way to our table, and Brix stood to hug her. As they got reacquainted, my phone chimed with a text. I pulled it out to see it was from Nate. Although we hadn't gotten as physically close as we did the night before the wedding, we kept in touch and spoke to one another often.

What's popping, superstar? I saw your shots in the Nordstrom ad. You looked good as hell, baby. I wanted to see if you think I could see you again. I have tickets for a game in Houston. My mama can't make it, and I would love to see you there.

I smiled slightly at my phone and responded. *Hey, boo. I'm chilling in Nome with my peeps. Just got here about an hour ago. I saw your game Tuesday night. You did your thing. Let me know the exact dates, and I'll let you know. I would love to be there.*

When I put my phone away, I noticed I was the center of attention. "Umm... why are y'all staring at me?"

My mama rolled her eyes. "Because you were smiling. It's so beautiful, we all have to stop and stare."

It was my turn to roll my eyes. "I know it's beautiful, but thank you."

Brix chuckled. "I was telling your mom that I was hoping that you would come see what I did with the farm sometime tomorrow, and she invited me to the family turn up this weekend."

"Yeah, sure. We need to catch up anyway. I gotta spend tonight with my mama and daddy though."

My mom's face reddened, and she walked away. Whenever I called Carter daddy, it put them both in their feelings. He was my stepdad, and he only came along about six years ago, shortly before Joseph died. I bonded with him immediately, simply because he was everything my mother needed after all the abuse she suffered from Joseph. He nearly killed her at the end. That was why Uncle WJ shot his ass.

"I don't mean to pry, but I thought I heard your dad died a few years ago," Brix said with a slight frown on his face.

"He did. My mom remarried, and I have another brother. CJ bad as hell too."

"Damn. That's cool that you call him dad."

"Yeah. He deserves the title way more than Joseph did."

Brix cleared his throat as my phone chimed again. I could see that he was slightly uncomfortable with what I said. He knew about some of the horrible things Joseph would say and do to me. I would often go to him for comfort after school... well, when he didn't have a girlfriend. It was like he helped me to feel loved. As friends, Brix and I loved each other. I just hated that we let the dating scene distance us from one another.

I looked down at my phone to see another text from Nate. I smiled slightly as Brix asked, "You seeing somebody? Whoever is texting you must be pretty special."

"I'm not seeing anyone. Nate and I are friends. He's just cool. I haven't seen him since Nesha's wedding, but he wants me to go to one of his games since they'll be in Houston."

"Oh. The basketball player?"

"Yeah. He plays for Dallas."

He nodded, but it seemed that bothered him. He went back to eating his food, so I asked, "How long you been back in town?"

"Right after the New Year. So I was probably moving in right after you left from your last visit if you were here for Nesha's wedding."

"Yeah. We probably missed each other by a day or two."

He nodded again and went back to his food. When my phone chimed again, he glanced up at me but didn't stare like last time. This time, it was my girl Tyeis just checking on me. I responded to her, letting her know I was in the country and would call her later, then went back to my food. Brix was quiet, and I didn't know what to say to get conversation going between us again. He obviously wasn't as forward as he used to be. I could tell that he wanted me in ways he'd never had me, simply by the way his eyes scanned my body.

We needed to get reacquainted first though. Surely, neither of us were the same person we were at eighteen years old. That was already evident. I was more vocal than I was back then. It was like we'd switched personalities. "Brix, you good?" I asked.

He lifted his gaze to mine, and the seriousness in his eyes caused a tremble to go through my body. "I'm cool, Jess. I just have a lot of work to do, so my mind had gone there. I'm a planner and like to know what I'm gonna do before I do it."

My lips parted as he licked his while scanning my body again. Being the person I was now, I couldn't let him get away with that. "Brix, why do I get the feeling that those plans include me in some way?"

"Because you're a smart woman and can read between the lines. You ain't the same. You're bolder, and I can tell that you done been through some shit that made you tougher. I want to pursue you, Jess, but slowly. I want you to feel me in every way, but we gon' start with intellect. You cool with that?"

I frowned slightly then shrugged. "I guess... umm... Why are you suddenly interested?"

"Can I be honest?"

"That's the best thing, isn't it?"

I was starting to get a little irritated. It was like he was taking me on the scenic route of whatever it was he was really wanting to say. I was a straight shooter, and besides, I'd seen this route before, and I wasn't all that fond of it. He leaned over the table slightly. "I've always had a thing for you, but your father made it clear that you were off limits."

My eyebrows lifted. "You had a conversation with Joseph?"

"I wouldn't exactly call it a conversation. I was about to approach you at your induction into the National Honor Society. I'd sat in the back just to see you being honored. I was so proud of you. I'd planned to ask you to be mine that night. Your family had surrounded you, so you couldn't see me. He did though. He stopped me and said that you didn't have time for boys and for me to find me something else to do before I found myself covered in dirt. That's why we didn't talk much our senior year. It had nothing to do with my extra-curricular activities."

I swallowed hard, wondering about where my life would have gone if Brix and I had ended up together. I was thirty-one years old, nearly thirty-two. I was pretty sure back then that I would be married with my own family by this age. Knowing that Joseph probably had something to do with why I didn't only pissed me off. I would have given Brixton a shot at my heart. We were so cool back then... compatible in every way.

I glanced up at him and stood to get a to-go box. Normally, I would have cleaned my plate. That was why I didn't waste time by putting it in a to-go box in the first place. As I grabbed the box, Uncle Jasper walked in the restaurant with Uncle Storm behind him with all the signs. I slowly shook my head as Uncle Storm said, "Just so y'all know, Jasper was joking by putting all these signs out, but this is real as hell. I'm gon' be running for mayor of Big City Nome, Texas, and I'm gon' need y'all support. Real shit."

Everybody looked around at one another, probably wondering if he was serious or not. Finally, Mr. Spears stood from his seat and started clapping. Before long, everyone was on their feet. *Lord have mercy.* That was all the gas his ass needed. He smiled big and pushed Jasper away from him. If that fool didn't stand there and try to give an entire speech, then my name wasn't Jessica.

As I walked back to my table, my mama said, "Storm, get your ass out of here! This is not your election headquarters!"

He frowned at her, then it was like a lightbulb came on. "Oh, yes the hell it is! The diner, the barbershop, the tractor store, the washateria, Marcus's shop, and my shop will all serve as my damn headquarters. Y'all better fall in line before these winds tear y'all shit up. I need y'all to give me that push I need."

"Storm, you don't need all that for a population of fo' fitty, bruh. That's stupid," Uncle Jasper said. "Just put flyers in people's boxes at the post office and call that shit good."

Everybody laughed so hard. I tuned their crazy asses out and started boxing my food. Brix was laughing at their shenanigans until Uncle Storm followed my mama to the kitchen. I swore my uncle had too much time on his hands. Brix slid his hand over mine, causing me to look up at him, and said, "I need your number, baby. I know that shit popping, but I hope to have high priority status, at least while you're in town."

I unlocked my phone and gave it to him as it chimed. He smirked. "Nate wants to know if those dates are free for him. He really wants to see you and kiss your lips again. Hmph. Sounds like I have my work cut out for me."

I couldn't even respond to him as he called himself then saved his number in my phone. When he gave it back, I stood from my seat. "I'll call you tomorrow, Brix."

"Not if I call first. See you tomorrow."

My lips parted as I stared at him. After finally tearing my gaze away from him, I grabbed my box of food and made my way to my car. I took a deep breath then got in, trying to figure out why Joseph couldn't just stay dead. It was bad enough he haunted my dreams at times, but him being brought up in conversation with Brix was overwhelming. I hated that man, and I found that just because he was dead, it didn't make me free of his hold on me.

CHAPTER TWO

BRIXTON

Jessica Monroe was the sexiest woman I'd ever seen, even back when we were in school. Time had been good to her, and now that her father was out of the picture, I wanted to pursue something with her. When she walked into the diner, I swore Marvin Gaye had come back from the dead and started singing "I Want You". Had I not moved back to Nome, I probably would have given up on that. Once my dad got sick, I knew I would be coming back to take over things.

The Hendersons were more involved with business in the city than they were when I left, so I knew it would be harder to get things going. My people used to sell hay, and they bred animals to sell as well. Mr. Henderson had purchased cattle from my grandfather back when I was a kid. From what I understood from my mama, WJ Henderson had purchased cattle recently just to help them out. I could respect a man like that. I knew if I needed anything, I would be able to go to him for either advice or help.

I couldn't let everything my grandparents worked to build fall by the wayside like it meant nothing. Their blood, sweat, and tears were in this land. My grandfather had sewed every dollar he had into making this property an operable farm. My mama said Mr. Henderson had more money because he got in cahoots with some affluent white folks. He was also more aggressive than my grandfather.

She told me that some white folks back in the day had just moved on his land and claimed it as their own. Mr. Henderson refused to settle for that. Rumor had it that he'd killed a couple of them. Because of his backing, it was swept under the rug. My grandfather didn't have that 'I don't give a fuck' attitude that Mr. Henderson had. You almost *had* to have it back then to be successful.

When I left for college, things were okay. Business was steady enough to keep things afloat. However, before I graduated, my grandfather passed away, and a couple of years later, my grandmother died as well. My dad's health wasn't that great when he took over things. He was already battling diabetes and high blood pressure. According to his medical records, he was battling a couple of other illnesses I had no clue about.

He died last year from a heart attack at sixty-five years old. My mama was left in debt and a farm she had no clue how to run. My sister would be of no assistance to her as far as that went, unless she wanted to sell it. My sister was a realtor in New York. She made a decent living, so she paid some of dad's debts, and I paid the rest. Had he said something, we could have helped him take care of things before they added fees for defaulting.

By the time he passed, I'd gotten a master's degree in business and had opened my own gym in Austin. It had done well, and I was considering opening another in Houston right before he passed away. That idea had taken a back seat. Until I got the farm running like it should, that would be off the table. I also noticed that there wasn't a gym in the area, and it could be something I could give serious thought to adding. For an adequate gym, people mostly had to go to Beaumont.

As I left the diner, I saw Jessica pulling away. Our days in school were some of the best times of my life. She was an amazing friend, despite her father's antics. I didn't want to tell her that he'd kept me away from her, but I wasn't about to take the heat for what he'd done to keep us apart. I didn't tell her everything, but I told her enough.

That man was something else. All the shit he did to assure she was a subordinate to him and other men, was narcissistic, chauvinistic, and any other 'nistic' you could think of. He'd gone as far as watching me on his off days, making sure I had no contact with her. She thought because I was dating that I distanced myself from her. I wanted to be dating her. According to him, my family didn't have shit and wouldn't be able to take care of Jessica.

Jessica Monroe was her own woman now and surely didn't need a man to take care of her. However, I hoped she still wanted that though. She was the one I wanted and couldn't have. Things her dad said had kept me from pursuing her once she got away from under his thumb. I felt like I wasn't good enough for her. I'd seen her on several occasions when I came to town, but I made sure she didn't see me.

I didn't want any drama between her and her father because of her involvement with me. I pined over that woman for years, and now that I knew my worth and that I deserved her and everything she had to offer, she was occupied... too occupied. She said she and Nate were friends, but apparently, they were more if he'd kissed her. The way she was blushing and shit had said so as well. She said he was a basketball player, so I was pretty sure it was Nate Guillory if he played for Dallas.

I wasn't intimidated by anyone, but I needed to see where Jessica's head was at. She had options, but I needed to be sure I was one of them. I could tell she was thinking hard about what I said, and it had brought her down. I really wanted to just be there for her like the old days before her father got involved, but she didn't seem to want to be bothered. I was trying not to be too forward with her, because in the past, she didn't seem to like that. However, it seemed she lived for it now. I could tell she'd gotten irritated with me.

As I got in my truck and headed back to the house, my mama called. "Hello?"

"Hey, baby. Have you eaten? I didn't feel too good, so I didn't cook the meat I took out."

"Don't worry about that, Ma. I ate. Did you want me to pick you up something? Medicine, food, or anything?"

"I'm gonna eat soup, but if you don't mind stopping at the corner store and picking up some NyQuil, I'd appreciate it."

"Of course, Ma. I got'chu."

"Thank you, baby," she said, then coughed before hanging up.

When I got to the store, Jessica's uncle was in there, so I spoke. "How you doing, Mr. Henderson?"

I smiled slightly. "Kenny. Mr. Henderson is my dad or WJ's old ass."

He extended his hand, and I shook it as I chuckled. "I was sorry to hear about your dad. Mr. Lewis was a good man. I apologize for just getting a chance to say so personally."

"Thank you. We received the plant and gift card from the Hendersons. That was really thoughtful of you guys. Thank y'all for looking out for the community."

"We have been blessed and in a position to do so much. Why not start with the community we live in? It irritates me when people help everybody but their own. Big City Nome is our home and always will be. It's our job to take care of it."

I loved his disposition. Kenny was usually the quiet one. For him to say so much to me had to mean something. I nodded my head appreciatively and walked away to get the NyQuil. He turned back to me and said, "You know that goes for you too. Since the younger Hendersons are handling the rice and grass farms and the hay fields, I have a little time on my hands. I don't mind helping you. I see you out there every day."

"You don't know how much I'd appreciate that. That fence been tearing my ass up."

I slid my hand over my face as he put his hand on my shoulder. "Don't worry. I'll be out there tomorrow, if you're working."

"Yes, sir, I will be."

"Okay, man. See you tomorrow. Tell me your name again."

"Brixton, but everyone calls me Brix."

"Got it. See you bright and early."

He walked out of the store, and I was somewhat frozen in place. What were the odds that Kenny would offer to help me, and he didn't really know me? My grandparents' land wasn't far from his house, so I was sure he knew them and my father well. However, that didn't necessarily trickle down to me. I made my way to the register, thankful that I ran into him today, and paid for my mama's medicine, then made my way home.

When I got there and had given Mama her meds, I took a shower and had planned to chill out for the rest of the evening. However, I was pleasantly surprised when my phone chimed with a text message from Jessica. I opened the message with a slight smile on my face.

So, I've been thinking a lot since I left the diner. I hate Joseph for how he altered my life. The woman I became was a direct result of how he treated my mama and me. I don't settle for anything less than what I want... period. I'm not a submissive woman, and no man I've met has proven to me that I can be safe being submissive. I'm damaged, Brix. I just suffered a massive heartbreak right before Christmas, and I'm still working on myself to be okay with it.

Nate was there when I was vulnerable and drunk. That was how he felt my lips. While I don't feel like I owe you an explanation, at the same time, I feel like I do. We were such good friends and knowing that Joseph had something to do with why we faded apart, angers me. I can't even talk to my mom about this. I have to go back to counseling, because I find myself blaming her a lot for what I went through.

I read her message a few times, trying to debate if I wanted to respond through text or if I wanted to call. A slight smile made its way to my face as I thought about how I used to respond to her back in the day when she needed me. I typed the message out before I changed my mind and hit send. *Come to Brix, baby.*

I decided to add to it. *We don't have to talk if you don't want to. I just want to offer you comfort, like old times.*

I sat in the recliner, waiting for her response. When it didn't come, I turned on the TV to watch *9-1-1 Lone Star*. That sun had been whupping my ass. Going to the gym to work out was the last thing on my mind. I was drained. Hopefully, the assistance Kenny offered would help me finish a lot faster. I had the cattle in a smaller field, and they were gonna wear that grass out until there was nothing left if I didn't hurry with what I was doing.

I hadn't had to work on a fence in years... since I was a teenager. I took a swig of the water from the thermos I'd left next to my chair earlier today. After putting my feet up and starting the show, I could feel myself drifting. This was a waste of time. It was only seven thirty, and I was falling asleep. Just as I turned the TV off, the doorbell rang. While I was hoping it was Jessica, I wasn't totally sure. A man had come by earlier while I was working on the fence, talking about how my dad owed him money. I told him unless he had proof of that shit, that debt died with him.

I didn't bother checking the peephole, because just the thought of that had me irritated. My temper was oozing from my ears, thinking I would have to go off on his ass. I flung the door open to see Jessica standing there. She'd changed into some sweats and a T-shirt. I grabbed her hand and gently pulled her inside and into my arms. She wasn't crying, but I felt like it would only be a matter of time before she was.

She used to always tell me that she wasn't a crier, but I brought out her sensitive side. I hoped that still held true. I closed the door and locked it, then pulled her back to me. She took a deep breath as we stood there. I kissed her forehead and asked, "You wanna go watch TV?"

"No. I want to talk."

That shocked me. I nodded and led her to the couch in the room I was sitting in, and when I sat next to her, she lay against me, rubbing her hand over my chest. She used to always do that shit, and it had the same effect on me as it did back then. I was starting to brick up. I grabbed her hand and kissed it then just held it in mine. I couldn't be all hard and shit while she talked. I wouldn't hear a word she said.

"So this happened at the National Honor Society induction or the National *Junior* Honor Society induction?"

"What's the difference?"

"One was in middle school, and the other was in high school."

"It happened at both, actually. I mean... he just told me to stay away from his daughter when we were in middle school. What I told you earlier happened in high school. I wanted to be with you so bad by then, but I knew I would have to wait until we were grown."

She lifted her head and stared at me for a moment. Lifting her hand, she slid it through my beard as she stared into my eyes. "So you were falling for one of your best friends, Brix?"

"I was in love with my *best* friend, not one of. No one compared to you, Jess."

I slid my fingertips over her cheek. She looked away and lay back against my shoulder. "Brix, my mama could tell something was wrong. I know she's gonna want to talk. I don't want to tell her how I'm feeling about her."

"Then don't. Just tell her about Joseph. She doesn't have to know what you're dealing with concerning her. There's nothing she can do about that now. I'm not saying your feelings aren't valid, but it's just tough."

"I know. I love my mama, but damn. Why did she have to put up with his ass for so long? The man she's married to now wanted to take her away from him when I was five years old. She was cheating, and that's when Joseph first hit her. It didn't stop after that. He even hit me a couple of times and masked it as discipline for me talking back. I hated him so much. As soon as I could get out of there, I did. He was pissed, too, but I wouldn't let him stop me."

"I'm sorry you had to go through that, baby. You never told me he hit you."

I could feel the frown grace my features. I was getting angry about something that probably happened fifteen to twenty years ago and by a dead man. "I didn't want you to try to defend me. The first time it happened, I was only eleven. He said I was too smart mouthed. I always thought I inherited that from Aunt Tiffany or Uncle Storm, but I found out that my mother used to be the same way before she got caught up with Joseph."

Apparently, Joseph had beat all the fun out of her because all I remembered was Mrs. Jenahra going to church all the time. I could only shake my head at her revelation. I didn't know how she made it in that house. Jacob, her brother, got to do whatever he wanted, but anytime Jess wanted to go somewhere, she had to act like she was going to a female friend's house. She would literally drive over there, and I would pick her up.

That all stopped the summer before twelfth grade after her induction into the National Honor Society. That man was evil. I'd heard that her mom had killed him, so I asked to be sure. "Your mom killed him?"

"Yeah," she said as she shifted. "He was beating the shit out of her because she had reconnected with Carter and found the courage to just leave. I think she felt protected with Carter, like Joseph wouldn't be able to get to her if he was around. Joseph had come home early and caught her packing. Had she not killed him, he definitely would have killed her."

"How was she able to get away to get a gun?"

She shifted again. Something was up. "I don't know. I didn't ask for details."

"She didn't do it, did she?" I asked.

I could always tell when she was lying. She would start fidgeting. She looked up at me, silently pleading with her eyes. "No, but she took the wrap. You can't say anything."

"You know I would never say a word."

"My uncles showed up, because Jacob had gone to Granny's house, and Mama was taking too long to join him. Plus, Aunt Aspen had witnessed Joseph manhandling her at Aunt Chrissy's wedding. She told Uncle Storm, although my mom had begged her not to. It took her a few days to tell him, but it seems she told him right on time, because they went down there… all four of them to witness him beating the shit out of her. Uncle WJ killed him."

I nodded repeatedly. Her Uncle WJ and her mom were pretty close. Mrs. Jenahra had done a good job at hiding the abuse she was going through. He should have picked up on it long before it got to that point though. I pulled Jessica back to me and held her close. "So tell me about the man that broke your heart, baby."

I gently slid my hand up and down her arm, trying to soothe her. I could feel her trembling. I couldn't believe this shit about Joseph was still tormenting her. She used to tremble like this all the time when she talked about him. Rehashing everything had the same effect on her. "There isn't much to tell. We were together for a year, but for the last four months of it, I felt like I was in a relationship alone. I broke up with him. He was Nesha's brother-in-law, unfortunately. He still calls from time to time to tell me he loves me, although neither of us said it while we were together."

I frowned. "Y'all were together a year and had never said that you loved each other?"

"No. When I wanted to say it was when his behavior started changing, so I kept it to myself. He decided to tell me after we broke up that he loved me all along. I promised him that he wouldn't get me back by telling me that, but he continues to say it anyway. I wondered if he loved me when he cheated."

I held her tighter to me. She was masking a lot of hurt. Just the fact that she was talking to me about it made me feel like we still had that special bond we had in school. She stared up at me for a moment, then grabbed my beard, pulling me to her, and gave me a tender kiss on the lips. "Thank you for listening to me, Brix. You were always a really good friend."

I pulled her back to me and kissed her again, allowing it to linger a bit. "I wanna be more than a friend now, Jess. I know you have a lot of shit going on right now, but I'm gon' be here for you... always. I ain't going nowhere this time."

She didn't respond to me. She laid her head against me, and within minutes, she'd fallen asleep. *The more things changed, the more they stayed the same.*

CHAPTER THREE

JESSICA

"*Maybe if you make her back her big ass away from the table, she could lose some weight. She's gonna be as big as your sister.*"

"*Our daughter is a beautiful young woman, Joseph, and so is Chrissy. Her size doesn't matter.*"

"*No daughter of mine is gonna be walking around looking like she done swallowed a whole ass Buick! Do something or I will!*"

My eyes popped open, and I realized I was still laying against Brixton. *Shit.* What was I still doing here? I came here and spilled all my damn emotions and messed around and fell asleep. Talk about déjà vu. When I was sixteen, I'd come here to talk about Joseph and was supposed to be at my homegirl's house. I had fallen asleep and missed curfew by an hour. Thankfully, Joseph had fallen asleep as well, or I would have gotten my ass whupped.

I sat up, and Brix did too. "I didn't want to wake you up. I figured if you fell asleep, you must have needed the rest."

I gave him a tight smile then stretched. Looking at my phone, I saw it was just about midnight. I had to have slept a couple of hours. He'd judged me right, because I was definitely tired after only getting about three hours of sleep early this morning. "I'm sorry, Brix. I didn't mean to fall asleep. I'll call you in the morning. Okay?"

"You don't have to leave, Jess. We're not kids anymore."

It felt like I was after that dream. I hated dreaming about his ass. It seemed the counseling I went through after his death was for naught. The dreams had never stopped, but in true Jessica fashion, I'd made it look easy. No one knew the turmoil I was in and why it was hard for me to trust people. I couldn't trust my own father.

I stared Brix in the eyes as he caressed my cheek. "You're so beautiful, Jess. Time has been so good to you."

I smiled slightly. "It's been good to you too."

"Naw. You see these crow feet around my eyes?"

I giggled. "That's not crow feet, boy. That's just how your eyes are, especially when you're feeling sensitive."

His eyebrows lifted. "What makes you think I'm feeling sensitive?"

"You always are when I'm around, spilling all my fucking emotions on you. I thought things would be different since we hadn't talked in so long, but just like old times, I felt comfortable telling you things I haven't told a soul."

That shit was weird as hell. I never even told Decklan about my upbringing. People just assumed it was great because I didn't give them a reason to think that it wasn't. They saw I was connected to the Henderson family, so things couldn't have been too bad. The Hendersons were known for their wealth and status. They were also known for being good people. If they only knew the half.

For the most part, my mama and her siblings *were* good people, and my grandparents were now too. It wasn't always that way though. Secondly, the Hendersons had nothing to do with the recent drama from the Monroes and the Boltons. The Boltons were Aunt Chrissy's first set of in-laws. Her first husband had molested my cousins. He was probably one step away from molesting me too. He used to look at me weird all the time. I was so developed for my age though. That was what probably kept me safe. I didn't look like a little girl.

Brix pulled me close and kissed my forehead. His kisses were everything. This was my first time feeling his lips against mine this way though. When he pulled me back to him and kissed me, I wanted to slide my tongue to his. That was my vulnerability leading the way. That was the mistake I'd made with Nate. Thankfully, this time I wasn't drunk and was able to contain myself.

"I've carried your soul in mine for years, baby. When I picked up the nerve to contact you, you were involved with someone. I convinced myself that you had long forgotten about me and that I needed to move on too. In my mind, I felt like you were feeling me, too, and I realized that was something that I had imagined... hoped."

I looked away from him for a moment, reminiscing about the time we shared. "I had a slight crush, but you were my friend. I didn't know you were feeling that way. Why did you have to pick up the nerve to contact me?"

"It had been so long since we'd talked. I didn't think you would be receptive."

Just like he knew when I was lying, I knew he was lying now too. "Tell me the truth, Brix."

He took a deep breath and slid his hand over his mouth. "Joseph said I wasn't good enough for you. My family was struggling, and his daughter deserved better. You deserved someone who would be able to take care of you."

"Fucker," I mumbled. "You ever wondered where we would be had he not interfered?"

"I don't wonder. I know. You would be my wife and the mother of my kids by now. That shit is going to take a lot more convincing now though."

"You're off to a great start," I whispered.

Brix grabbed my chin and turned my face to his. He didn't hesitate when he laid his lips on mine. He was taking what he wanted, and that shit turned me on more than a little bit. When he deepened the kiss and slid his hand to my waist, my body trembled. *This is Brix, bitch! Your best friend in school.* My thoughts were trying to make me stop this, but we were far removed from high school. I couldn't stop.

His tongue slid to mine, and I couldn't help but moan into his mouth. It didn't seem like he was going to be taking things as slow as he'd said, unless he was teasing me. His hand slid down further to my hip, and my middle had begun to pulsate. However, when I heard a noise, I pulled away from him to see his mother coming down the hallway.

Her nose was red, and she had tissue in her hand. When she looked up and saw me, her eyes widened. "Jessica?"

"Yes, ma'am," I said as I stood.

She smiled big. "I would hug you, but I'm sick as a dog. I would hate to pass this to you."

"I take vitamin C. I need a hug."

I went to her and hugged her tightly. This woman always treated me like a daughter, and she provided what I was missing from my own mother at times. When I saw her telling her husband off and giving him the business, that was foreign to me. I just knew he was going to go upside her head. When that didn't happen, I was in a different world. All I knew was the relationship between Joseph and my mother.

When I released her, she smiled again. "I'm so glad the two of you reconnected," she said as she glanced at Brixton.

I glanced at him, too, and responded, "Me too."

WHEN I WOKE UP, I realized that I'd somehow made it to the bed. I didn't remember getting in the bed. I was confused like I'd taken something to go to sleep. That was probably just how good I slept. I'd never been so comfortable in someone else's bed. I wondered if Brix had slept in here with me. Before I could even get out of bed, my phone vibrated on the nightstand. When I picked it up, I realized I had a few text messages.

I rarely put my phone on vibrate, so I was more than sure Brixton had done that. I saw that the incoming call was from my mama, so I answered. "Hello?"

"Jess, baby, I'm worried about you. Are you okay? Where did you sleep last night?"

"Hey, Mama. I'm okay. I stayed at Brixton's place. I just woke up."

"Well, I take it that the two of you have gotten reacquainted. Has he changed much?"

"He seems a little more considerate. He's not as forward as he used to be. I don't know if that's just until we get more acquainted with who we are as adults or if that change is permanent. I suppose time will tell."

"Are you sure you're okay, baby? You sound so nonchalant."

"I'm okay. I'll see you in a little bit. It smells like Brix is cooking breakfast."

"Okay. Talk to you soon."

I got up from the bed and went to the bathroom to rinse my mouth out then made my way to the kitchen. When I saw Brix standing at the stove shirtless, I nearly drooled on myself. As I approached him, he turned to me and asked, "What's up, sleepy head? You slept like a log last night. I could have *thrown* you in the bed and you wouldn't have woken up."

"Oh, whatever. I wasn't sleeping that hard."

"Shiiiid. You were snoring the paint off the walls."

"First of all, nigga, I don't snore. Secondly, I don't remember a damn thing after hugging your mother and going back to the couch."

He laughed. I didn't have a dream. That was unusual, but I was thankful at the same time. That feeling only prompted the next question. "Did you sleep in the bed with me?"

"Mm hmm. Held your beautiful ass in my arms all night. That's how I know you were snoring."

He chuckled as I side-eyed him. "You don't know shit."

I couldn't stop my eyes from scanning his body. *Shit!* Brix had been working out like crazy. His body was massive... muscles bulging on every inch of it. For some men, that looked like overkill, but on his six feet two inches, it looked mouthwatering. Apparently, I got mesmerized because I didn't even notice he was staring at me. "You like what you see, Jess?"

I blinked rapidly, breaking myself from the trance I was in. "Uhh... yeah. You fine as shit. You making me wanna get in the gym."

That's a got damn lie. My thickness was something that drove men to me, despite Joseph's assessment of me. Men loved this shit, and by the time I got to college, I really found that shit out. However, I had never had a problem pulling a nigga, but to pull one as sexy as Brix had taken my damn confidence into dangerous territories.

"Naw. This body need to stay just like it is," he said as he approached me. He slid his arm around my waist and pulled me close to him. "Feeling this softness against me last night almost had me taking advantage of yo' fine ass."

"Hmm. Maybe you should have," I said as my face heated up.

I couldn't be saying no shit like that. When I looked away from him, he grabbed my chin and turned my face back to him. "I said I was gonna go slow wit'chu, but if you gon' be talking like that, the only time I'm gonna go slow is when I'm stroking that pussy, Jess."

He took my fucking breath away. The forward nigga I'd known when we were in school was still there. I slid my hand behind his head and roughly pulled his face to mine. My tongue sought out his as we kissed roughly. It was like the desire had over manifested, and I couldn't turn it off, especially not after he grabbed my ass with both hands, lifting that shit, and lowered his face to my neck.

He bit my skin there as I moaned slightly. When I felt the stiffness against me, I wanted to immediately drop to my knees to give him what I knew he loved. We talked about all kinds of shit when we were younger, and I knew he absolutely loved good head. If he got that, he could wait on actual sex. I used to tease him and tell him that his stroke game must have been lacking. I was willing to find out right here in this kitchen though.

Taking a deep breath, Brix wrapped his arms around my waist. He was pulling back and halting us before we really got cranked up. That was probably best. His mother was here. The last thing I needed her seeing was us hot and heavy in the place she ate her food. I was more than sure he wouldn't want her seeing him while his dick was hard either. I pulled away from him, and my eyes immediately traveled there. His ass put the stereotype to rest. *Shit!*

I used to hear women say all the time that men who were muscular had small dicks because most of them were on steroids. Brix's dick hadn't lost any steam. I'd seen it once in high school and nearly lost my damn mind... not in front of him, of course. The crazy part was that he'd just stood there in his nakedness and smirked at me, and said, *"See what these hoes after, girl?"*

I'd rolled my eyes and walked off, knowing that my virgin kitty had gotten weak with desire for something she'd never had. I had to go to the girls' locker room and take a cold shower to calm my hot ass down. Brix was my friend, and I couldn't be fiending over his ass like that. Had I known he was feeling me like he was, I would have given him my innocence quick as hell. The muthafucka I gave it to didn't deserve it, and nobody deserved that piece of dick he had the audacity to lie on.

I learned a valuable lesson, fucking around with him: A nigga that bragged on his shit usually pissed on his balls. I barely even felt that shit, and I was a damn virgin. *How the fuck?* My cherry didn't get popped until I found some shit worth being called a dick, and that was in college. Without my parents' watchful eyes, I fucked around a lot. Thankfully, Joseph didn't find out about me when I was at home.

In small towns, everyone knew everybody, but Joseph was an outsider. Nobody really talked to him like that, except at church. If they knew anything about my behavior, they didn't tell. They probably just gossiped about me. Had Joseph known I was no longer a virgin, he probably would have beat my ass then made sure I didn't leave the house.

Without a word, Brix turned back to the stove and started plating our breakfast as I stared at his ass, imagining myself pulling him deeper inside of me. I closed my eyes, trying to rid myself of the thoughts, then pulled my phone from my pocket. I saw the messages still there and decided to read them to get my mind off Brix slow fucking me. When I saw Decklan's name, I rolled my eyes but still opened his message to see what he wanted.

Hey, Jess. I hope you've had a good day, baby. I miss you. I popped up at your place and you weren't there. When you get back, please call me. I need to talk to you.

I couldn't believe he'd popped up at my house. His ass had plenty of audacity. Usually, it was muthafuckas that fucked up that had all the audacity in the world. I went to the next message to see what else he possibly had to say after that.

Are you in Nome? I thought I heard Nesha saying something about you being in town. Maybe I can come there to talk to you. Please, Jess. I need you. I love you.

The tremble made its way through my body. Anger was coursing through me because I wanted him to stop trying so hard. I was done. Despite how much I loved him, I knew that he was no good for me. He didn't try to rectify his behavior until I got tired of dealing with the shit. I responded to him as my face twitched in anger.

Do not show up here. If you do, your feelings gon' get hurt.

As petty as I was, I would be all over Brix in his face and not give a fuck... just like I didn't give a fuck when Nate was trying to be up in my sauce. Decklan was no longer my concern; that included his pitiful ass feelings. I had two more messages. One was from Nate. I'd looked at my schedule and had agreed to go to the game in two weeks. I'd just be getting back from a shoot in the Bahamas.

I opened his message to see, *Hey, beautiful. Can you call me when you have time?*

That was last night. I was here and had fallen asleep. My last message was from my mother. I didn't bother reading it since we'd already talked. I looked up at Brix as he set a plate of food in front of me. When I saw shrimp and grits, that shit caught me off guard. I stared up at him. "Damn. You can cook now?"

"Hell yeah, girl. I'm a jack of all trades now. I took a few culinary classes. Fuck wit'cho boy."

I chuckled and glanced at my phone again. "Did you put my phone on vibrate last night?"

He sat across from me and bit his bottom lip. "Yep. You was knocked the hell out, and I wanted you to rest. That shit was going off back-to-back. You were exhausted, baby."

He grabbed my hand and began blessing our food while I stared at him in awe. When he was done, he stared up at me. "Eat up, baby."

My lips parted, and I grabbed my fork to taste this meal. It looked and smelled amazing. I just hoped it tasted as good as it looked. After my first forkful, I closed my eyes and moaned. It was so damn good. When I opened my eyes, Brix had scooted closer to me. He grabbed my fork and began feeding me more as he stared into my eyes. This shit was intense. After swallowing, I said, "Brix."

"Mm hmm."

"Are you trying to seduce me?"

"Do you feel like you're being seduced? I mean, all that don't feel necessary to me since you already receptive, baby. If my mama wasn't up there sleeping, I would have you bouncing all over this dick right now, screaming my name." He scooted closer to me and said in a low voice near my ear, "Then I'd slow fuck you while staring into your eyes so I could get acquainted with your soul. Mm. Tell me you wouldn't let me do that shit."

I did my best to remain quiet like he wasn't affecting me as much as he was, but that shit was impossible. "Brix, it feels like I'm being seduced and teased at the same time. Don't fucking play with me. Your mama will walk in here and find your dick in my mouth."

I closed my eyes, imagining myself digesting all his descendants. "Fuck, girl. Keep fucking with me and that's where you gon' find me... balls deep in your throat, fucking your esophagus up. I wanna wait until your heart is right though. I want you to fall in love with more than my dick."

When I heard footsteps, I cleared my throat and scooted away from him. It was a good thing he was still living here with his mother. Had he not been, we would have fucked last night, and my heart would have regretted it. A fuck was a fuck, and emotions usually didn't matter. However, Brix wanted more. He deserved more than what I had to offer right now, so what I had to offer would be off the table until I felt the same things he did.

CHAPTER FOUR

BRIXTON

I stood in the mirror and made sure I looked good. I'd worn some Rockstar jeans, a long-sleeved printed shirt I'd gotten from Cavender's, and a nice pair of boots. I was ready as hell to have fun at the Henderson family party. I was happy Mrs. Jenahra invited me, because I couldn't wait to see Jessica again. After yesterday morning, I didn't talk to her anymore until I sent a text saying goodnight.

Kenny had come over, and we'd worked all day on that fence. Jasper had stopped by on his way home and helped out as well. It helped that I had someone running the auger so I could set the poles. Since we didn't finish, Kenny said he would bring their auger next time. It would save us a lot of time. Being that I was busy, I really didn't have time to chase down Jess anyway. When I texted her, she only said *good night* in response.

I hopped in my Dodge and made my way to their family barn right up the highway from my grandparents' house. I guess I should call it my mother's house since it had been passed down to her. When I got to the barn, the party was already in full swing. I didn't think I was that late, but I guess I was. The zydeco music was blasting, and I could hear people talking over it. When I walked through the door, Kenny noticed me right away.

Jasper and Storm followed behind him, Storm with his usual frown. "What's up? I see you made it," Kenny said.

"Yep. I couldn't dare turn down an invitation to turn up with the Hendersons."

Storm's face eased up as he said, "Hell naw, you couldn't. I'm glad you gon' be here for my announcement."

"Aww, nigga. Ain't nobody give a shit about that. Brixton here because he tryna become our nephew," Jasper said.

Storm's frown came back as he stared at me. He and Jess were close. She'd told me as much. I knew they would all be protective of her because of her last heartbreak. "One day. I'm not rushing. As long as we're progressing, then I'm good," I said as Jessica approached.

She grabbed my hand and pulled me away from them to a table. "I am not about to let them grill you like I'm not a grown ass woman."

I chuckled, but once we sat, I could feel the tension. She turned to me and said, "Normally, I wouldn't have said a thing, but I at least owe you a warning. I'm about to be extremely petty from Petty University, majoring in pettiology."

I frowned, trying to figure out what the hell she was talking about. "What?"

"That muthafucka brought his ass to the country anyway, and now he's about to get his feelings hurt. I'm glad we had our intimate moments yesterday morning, because if we hadn't, you would think everything I'm gonna do tonight was fake. I just wouldn't be doing all this shit in front of everybody."

"All what shit?" I asked.

I glanced around, trying to figure out who she was talking about. She grabbed my beard, answering my question silently, and pulled my face to hers and kissed me on the lips. She didn't have to worry about me, because I could be just as petty as her. If somebody here was fucking up her vibe, she knew I would have her back. I grabbed her hand and pulled her from her seat to me and continued pulling her until she was on my lap.

When I did was when I noticed him. He was sitting near Nesha and her husband, and he looked pissed. "I'm gon' be doing the most. I hope you're not easily embarrassed, Brix."

"When it comes to you and this beautiful body, there ain't much you can do to embarrass me. I'll fuck you right here in front of your family."

She turned to me, and I noticed her cheeks had reddened. Maybe I would be the one embarrassing her ass. I wrapped my arms around her waist, but she stood from my lap. Grabbing my hand, she pulled me, so I stood. "I'm sure you want to eat. You know we have the works. I haven't eaten yet, because my mood was fucked. For the life of me, I still don't know why he showed his ass up here."

"Well, I believe we're about to find out, because he's making his way over here."

She turned toward him with a deep frown on her face. I swore she looked like her uncles when she frowned. When he got close, he nodded at me. I didn't reciprocate. Although this was petty bullshit to Jess, in my mind, she was already mine. When I didn't reciprocate, he cleared his throat. "Jess, can I talk to you?"

"Hell no. You shouldn't even be here, and you're being rude."

"I didn't mean to be rude. You know that."

He glanced at me again as I wrapped my arm around Jessica's waist then walked away. I was confused as to why he would even approach her while she was with another nigga anyway, talking about he didn't mean to be rude. His entire approach was rude as fuck. We continued to the steam tables, and when I saw that deer meat, I was in heaven. She glanced at me then grabbed the tongs to begin fixing our food.

I held my plate while she loaded me up. Despite that nigga popping up here, I could tell that her feelings were still on her sleeve concerning him. "You good, Jess?"

She only nodded as she put a scoop of rice dressing next to my deer sausage. My hand remained at the small of her back as we made our way down the line, with her putting a little of everything on my plate. Once we got back to our seats, I noticed Jess was somewhat quiet. Before I could address it, she grabbed my fork and began feeding me like I'd done her yesterday morning. I scooted closer to her. "You know you don't have to put on a façade for me. I can tell you still have feelings for him. You know I will give you whatever you need."

She lowered her head then looked back up at me. "Can we go outside?"

"I got'chu, baby."

I grabbed her hand and led her outside to my truck. After grabbing the blanket from the back seat, I spread it out in the bed and helped her up there. Once she got situated, I passed our food to her from the side of the truck then went to the tailgate and hopped in and sat next to her. She turned to me and said, "This is nice, Brix. Thank you."

I gave her a slight smile as she ate some of her rice. "This is actually kind of romantic. I didn't think you had it in you," she said.

"There's still quite a bit you need to learn about me. One of those things is that I'm a grown muthafucka, and I behave accordingly. You need tenderness right now. I'm trying to provide what I believe you need."

She set her plate beside her and made her way to my lap. I set my plate down as well and wrapped my arms around her. She took a deep breath. "It's been over three months, and he won't leave me alone. How am I supposed to move on if he won't respect my boundaries? I need peace away from him."

"Make him respect them. If you have to call the police, then do that. Tell Nesha to tell her husband to stop letting him come around."

"He's probably the one helping him, hoping that he'll get me back."

"Well, you'll have to talk to them too. I think it will stop if they know how serious you are about moving on."

While I was giving her advice and being here for her comfort, I couldn't help but remember that Nate was still in the picture. She wanted to move on, but that didn't necessarily mean that she wanted to move on with me. Showing her tenderness when she was feeling a way was nothing new. Although we hadn't seen one another in years, this interaction was familiar. The deep kissing and groping weren't, but it wasn't hard to fall into that.

From what I gathered from conversation and simply from paying attention to her was that she was a sexual being. I believed she was in high school, too, but she had to keep it under wraps. I knew she wasn't a virgin by the time we graduated. I never hid my sexuality from her, even when it wasn't directed at her. So it didn't shock me that we'd ended up in the positions we were in. Had I not been living back at home with my mother, it would have gone down Thursday night.

Her lips were so fucking soft. I didn't want to stop kissing her. We'd kissed before but as friends, similar to the first peck she'd given me. When I kissed her again, I almost expected her to resist somewhat, because the old Jessica played hard at times, like shit didn't get to her. I knew better though.

I gently rubbed my hand up and down her back for a moment, until she left my arms' confines to sit back next to me. She grabbed her plate and went back to eating, so I did the same. "Jess! You out here?"

I turned to look through the back window and windshield of my truck to see who was looking for her. Once I saw who it was, I turned back to Jess. "That's your aunt Tiffany."

"I know. I recognized her voice."

"You aren't going to answer?"

"Yeah." She turned her head slightly and yelled back. "I'm over here, Aunt Tiff, on the back of the Dodge truck."

I could hear Tiffany's footsteps get closer as I took a bite of my barbeque chicken. When she got to the tailgate, she smiled. "I was worried about you. Hey, Brixton."

"What's up, Tiff?"

"Too much and nothing at the same time," she said, then giggled. Turning her attention to Jessica, she asked, "You okay? I mean, I can see you're being taken care of, but if you wanna talk later, you know I'm always available."

"I know. Thanks, Aunt Tiff, but I'm good."

Jessica glanced at me, and Tiffany smiled. "Okay. Well, see y'all later."

When she walked away, Jessica stared up at me. I licked my lips as I stared back. *Damn.* I wanted her so bad, but I knew we needed to wait. I wanted to ask if she was going to meet Nate for his game, but I didn't want to seem like I was all in her business. So, I steered the conversation in a slightly different direction. "How long will you be in town?"

"I leave Wednesday evening to go back to Houston. Then I fly to the Bahamas for a photo shoot. I'll be there for a few days, then I'll be back in Houston. I decided to go to Nate's game."

Since she brought it up, I didn't have to ask. I knew I could have, but I didn't want him on her mind. "So we better make good use of the time we have, right?"

She brought her hand to my cheek and gently stroked it but didn't respond verbally. We had a connection. I could feel the magnetism whenever I looked into her eyes. I knew she could feel it too. She'd have to be heartless not to feel it. "I'm going to church with Mama, Daddy, Jacob, and CJ tomorrow. It's supposed to be our family day. We're going to dinner after church. Monday, I'm supposed to be spending time with Nesha, Jakari, and Decaurey."

I nodded, wishing I could just kidnap her ass and hold her hostage. "And Tuesday?"

"Turn up Tuesday at Uncle Jasper's, because it's going up on a Tuesday." She rolled her eyes. "His words, not mine. You're more than welcome to come with me... that is if you don't mind being around smoke. It's gon' be a lot of puff, puff, pass around that muthafucka. Wednesday, I'll just be everywhere, trying to see everyone before I leave."

I needed to definitely take advantage of our alone time. I wouldn't get much of it. "Can you stay with me tonight? It seems this will be the only time I'll get to have with you."

"I'll make time, Brix. Even if it's just for that bomb ass breakfast."

"See, now I feel used," I said as she laughed.

"Hey! I need y'all inside for my announcement!"

We both rolled our eyes. *Storm and his bullshit.* Jessica huffed loudly. She smiled as she turned to me. "I will gladly stay with you tonight. I've missed you over the years. I'm going to soak up as much as I can of you. How will your mom feel about that?"

"Girl, my mama loves you. She always wanted us to hook up... be together. But we have the opportunity now. I'm not gonna rest until I've exhausted everything within me. I'm already yours, Jess. I just need you to eventually be mine, baby. Everything is in place. I'm just waiting on you and what you really want to be revealed. I'm not rushing you though. I'm just letting you know that I'm ready."

She closed her eyes, and a lone tear escaped her. She quickly wiped it away and scooted to the tailgate and slid out, leaving me alone to grab our leftovers. I took a deep breath and got out, throwing our food away on my way back inside. I looked around but didn't see her. I leaned against the wall as Storm went to the microphone. "Jenahra, bring yo' ass out that kitchen. Everybody need to know you on board with this."

As Mrs. Jenahra emerged and rolled her eyes, I noticed Jessica come out of the bathroom. She walked over to her stepfather and sat next to him. I'd pressured her without meaning to. She just wanted to be right now, and it probably seemed like I was trying to force her into more. I wasn't doing that. I just wanted her to know where I stood. I supposed it seemed like I was pressuring her in a way since I knew she was already aware of my position. I'd told her Thursday night.

I just wanted her to trust me enough to lose all her inhibitions.

Just lose her reservations with me. I would never let her down, and I knew she knew that. Her body was screaming for me to take care of her, but the fear in her heart seemed to be screaming louder right now. I knew she needed time to get over whatever it was she was fighting with. She just refused to talk about what her real fears were. I'd give her whatever she wanted without hesitation, but it didn't matter if she didn't trust me to do just what I said I would do.

"Now that all y'all got yo' ass in a seat, I can make my announcement. Abney is in a whole shit storm coming this election season. I'm running against his ass. He trusted me to handle things while he was sick, but that was the wrong move, because now I know the inside shit y'all don't have a clue about. I'm coming to set all that shit straight, and I need y'all to be with me on it. My headquarters will be at Jen and Chrissy's Diner. They get the most traffic, and I need to convince as many voters as possible."

Almost everyone in attendance was doing other shit. Hardly anybody was looking at him, and he noticed. He frowned. "As soon as I'm elected, I'm coming for all y'all asses. I'm gon' abuse the fuck out of the power they give me. Remember that! If I don't win, it's gon' be just as bad. Shit, with all my family's vote, I should be a shoe in. Ain't but four hundred muthafuckas out here."

When Mrs. Henderson stood, everyone's attention went to her. She walked up to the podium with Storm. He put his arm around her and gave her the mic. "Seven, I'm with you, but watch your language in front of these kids, baby."

"I'm sorry, Mama. I got pumped up. It's their fault for ignoring me."

Finally, another guy I knew from back in the day stood and said, "I got'chu, bruh."

"In case y'all didn't know, us two youngest Hendersons finna takeover Nome. Marcus gon' be there with me."

I frowned slightly. I didn't remember there being another Henderson sibling after Storm. That shit must've come out while I was gone. I could clearly see now that he was related. He had similar features. That nigga used to raise hell in Nome and at Hardin Jefferson High School. Maybe the secrecy behind who he really was was part of the reason.

He stood next to Storm and slapped his hand. "We 'bout to be like Chris Rock and Bernie Mac in this muthafu... Y'all get the point," Storm said as his mother nudged him. "All those signs y'all were laughing at 'bout to go back up... except the Gabriel one, because I'm about to be an angel of war right now."

"Nigga, you the devil! Satan himself, but I got'chu," Jasper yelled, causing everybody to laugh.

"Y'all need to meet my muscle... I mean my staff. Of course, my beautiful wife, Aspen, is my publicist. The twins gon' work with her on that by finding out all the dirt I need on Abney and all the shit he didn't do while in office. Maui gon' be my spokesperson. People smile when they see her. SS gon' be my wingman."

"Daddy, what about me?" his youngest inquired.

I couldn't help but chuckle and slowly shake my head. This shit was finna be funny as hell. Storm was already over the top. That nigga was gonna be in campaign mode wherever he went. "Remy, you my bodyguard. Anybody look like they tryna get at me wrong, you gon' be the one to take care of it."

That lil boy flexed his muscles while everybody laughed. Storm kept talking, but I had zoned out as I stared at the beautiful woman across the way. She was slightly leaning against her stepdad, watching Storm be ignorant. The torment in her eyes was evident. I also realized that I wasn't the only one watching her. Her ex was watching her too. I couldn't really knock him for trying to get her back, but at the same time, he needed to respect her desires. He fucked up, and he needed to accept it and move around.

I could only hope that Jessica would stay with me like she said she would. Before leaving tonight, I would have to make sure I was clear. I would wait for all the time it took her to be good with herself. I was ready for love, but I wanted her to be ready to experience it again, too, without the weight of how it hurt her in the past.

At this point, I could only wait and respect her wishes while, at the same time, forcing her to verbally acknowledge I was here. As I watched her, our eyes finally met. Her gaze didn't waver and neither did mine. After a moment more, I nodded at her and walked out the door.

CHAPTER FIVE

JESSICA

"Brixton ass done bulked up for real! Damn! He looks good, Jess!"

"Yeah, he does."

I was sitting at the diner with Nesha, having lunch, but thinking about how I distanced myself from Brix the other night. I had too many emotions flowing through me with Decklan being there. I couldn't handle Brixton's sensitivity right now. Had I gone to his house, he would have had my ass bent over, taking dick like his good girl. I slightly rolled my eyes at the thought. He used to say that shit all the time. *Come be my good girl, baby.*

I used to get so damn jealous when he would say that to other girls, because I was dying for him to say it to me. Had Joseph not controlled my fucking life, he would have been saying it to me only. My mama had noticed a shift in my behavior, and I knew I needed to talk to her. Yesterday, I was quiet for most of our family time. Carter had taken us to J. Wilson's after church, and once we left there, we'd gone home and chilled out.

After talking to my mama and Jacob about my schedule and listening to Jacob talk about the family business and the boutiques he ran with Carter, I went to my room. My mama had remodeled every room in the house except mine and Jacob's. She wanted to get rid of the bad memories without having to buy another house, although Carter had offered to build another. She should have taken him up on that offer.

I felt like I was suffocating in that house. My room was where I spent a lot of time thinking about the turmoil Joseph was putting her through and the bullshit he was doing to me. I had no idea of the things he did behind my back, like the situation with Brix. I was sure that wasn't all he did. Being in that room wasn't helping, because memories of his abuse were all over the damn place. I was trying my best to forget about it, because I was living the life I'd always dreamed about.

I always thought I wanted to be a full-figured model like Tocarra, but Joseph had my self-esteem so damn low at one point, I didn't think I would crawl out of the hole he dug for me. Somehow, I did though. My life was great in all aspects, except my love life. Had it not been for what I had to endure, I may have turned out differently, so I was doing my best to convince myself that everything happened for a reason, and it happened just the way it was supposed to.

"Jess, I'm sorry about Decklan. I didn't know he was coming, and neither did Lennox."

My eyebrows lifted as Jakari pulled up a chair to eat lunch with us. "What's up, y'all?"

"Not too much," Nesha responded. "Just trying to get my girl Jess out of the funk she's in."

"Why you in a funk, Jess? When Brix got there last night, you forgot all about our asses. Then y'all disappeared for at least thirty minutes. Y'all together?"

"No, Jakari. We're just friends... just like we were in school."

"Bullshit. That man *been* wanting you. He definitely sees you as more than a friend. He was only at the party for you. It was like he didn't know anybody else... like his ass didn't go to school with me and Nesha too. All he saw was his Bestie Jessie."

I frowned at him. "Bestie Jessie? Nigga, what? That shit sound country as hell. Like I'm on the farm milking cows and shit."

Jakari laughed as I stared at him without cracking a smile. "That's what he used to call you when he was talking to me. He had said that he was breaking out that friend zone when we were in school, or he was gon' have to score while he was in there to get you to see him as more. I guess that shit never happened."

I rolled my eyes, although I wanted to cry. Instead of humoring him with a response, I stuffed some yams in my mouth. The food had to be the best part about coming home. I didn't cook much because I was always on the go. There was no sense in cooking all that for just me either. Although there were soul food restaurants in H-Town, none of them were Jenahra and Chrissy's country cooking.

I missed living in the country. City life was fun when you had someone to hang with, but I was alone most times unless my girl Tyeis was in town. She was a model, too, and worked for Carter and Shylou as well. She and I were their only full-figured models. That was done purposely. They didn't want the attention scattered over a bunch of women. They wanted to focus on getting our faces and bodies out there. Tyeis had even done hand commercials, and I'd done shoe ads that showed off my feet.

Changing the subject, I turned to Nesha and interrupted her conversation with Jakari. "You're telling me that neither of you had any idea Decklan was coming here?"

"None. I wouldn't let him blindside you like that. You handled it well though."

"I always make shit look easy," I mumbled. "I'm sick of that shit."

"What? We couldn't hear you, Jess," Jakari said.

"Nothing."

I glanced around the restaurant as Uncle Storm walked through the door, carrying a box. The twins were with him, and they came straight to our table and sat down. Nesha frowned at them. "Just because we're first cousins don't make y'all grown enough to sit in on our conversations."

They rolled their eyes, then Bali said, "Y'all ain't saying nothing we ain't heard before. Now carry on."

They were both into their phones right after. Jakari chuckled and asked, "So where we going tonight? Decaurey say?"

"Yeah. You know his ass always sniffing out a party or some shit to do. We're supposed to be going to Painting with a Twist and somewhere else he said. I done forgot. He wanted to go bowling, but I ain't tryna break my nails with this shoot coming up. I won't have time to get them redone without taking time from something or someone else."

"Someone else like who?" Bali asked. "It only takes an hour to get your nails done."

"From that fine body builder that was at the family party the other night, Bali. He was all into her, and she was trying to act like she wasn't feeling him as much at the end. If I could see the chemistry between them, I know Decklan could. Jess petty like future Mayor Storm Henderson, so I know she was doing all that shit to make Decklan jealous. It worked because that nigga was in his feelings big time," Noni said.

They were too grown for their own fucking good. "Listen, y'all all in my business like y'all nosy ass father. I ain't in the best mood right now, so I won't have a single problem fucking both of y'all up. Move around."

They rolled their eyes, but they got their narrow asses up from our table. Jakari chuckled. "You know you the only one they really listen to."

"That's because they know I will do just what I say I'm gon' do. I done whupped their lil asses a couple of times."

Before we could resume our conversation about our festivities for the night, Uncle Storm came to our table. He wore his normal frown as he asked, "Jess, why you threatening my kids?"

"Because they all in my fucking business like they my age. They need to mind the business that pays them... like yo' lil campaign."

His eyebrows went up for a second, then he frowned again. "Just like you checked them, I'm finna check you. I ain't *yo'* fucking age. Direct that attitude where it needs to go. And my *lil* campaign? Sound like a hater to me. As part of my campaign, their jobs are to get in everybody's business, no matter how wack it is. Na get yo' ass up and hug me, Jess."

I closed my eyes for a moment and reeled my feelings in, then stood and hugged him around his waist. "I'm sorry, Unc," I said sincerely.

He kissed my head then pulled me away from Nesha and Jakari. "What's up wit'chu? And I don't wanna hear no bullshit. Brix fucking with you?"

"Yeah, but in a good way. I just can't get my mind to trust him like my heart wants to. I need to properly get over my heartbreak and make sure that I ain't feeling shit for Nate."

"You still talking to that nigga?"

"Yeah, but I haven't seen him since the wedding. He's a good guy."

"Oh, so you have *too* many options. I can narrow that shit down for you real quick."

"Naw, future mayor. Can't have you on the wrong side of the law."

He chuckled and hugged me again. "Holla at me later."

"Okay."

When I sat back down and he'd spoken to Nesha and Jakari, he left. I was the center of attention it seemed, so I said, "Tell Lennox to check his brother. He told me he was gonna come, and I told him not to. He showed his ass up anyway. I'm so done with him. If I ain't gave him no play in over three months, he should know he ain't getting shit now."

"I'm sorry, Jess. I'll tell him. Is that all that's bothering you? It seems like there's more. You just seem so irritable. You're never really like that, and I'm worried about you."

"Yeah, Bestie Jessie. We worried about you."

I glanced over at Jakari's lame ass. "Nigga, shut the fuck up. Always trying to tease somebody. You need a woman."

"You damn right I do. Point one my way because a nigga practically in starvation mode. Yo' uncle and Nesha daddy a damn slave driver."

"Quit your lying, fool!" Nesha yelled.

They all worked in the family business. Sometimes I wished I did too. Maybe when I slowed down on modeling, I would move back. My brother seemed to enjoy it, and so did Nesha and Jakari, although he was tryna drag my uncle. "You gon' get off Uncle WJ. Unc is doing a hell of a job with the business. You better soak up all you can before he fully retires. You're the oldest Henderson grandson, so I'm more than sure all this shit finna be yours."

"Yeah, yeah, yeah. He said the same shit. Me and Philly been running shit, but I can tell he's on the downside of it too. Mal might be joining us on the business side of things soon though. Christian is more focused on A/C work with LaKeith. Most likely, he's going to be taking the lead on that when LaKeith is ready to slow down. Rylan only dips in from time to time. He's mostly working with Uncle Storm."

"Yeah. Jacob worked with him for a while, but he realized that wasn't his calling. After he'd been there for a few months, he was sick of looking at cars," I said and chuckled.

Our little brothers were doing their best to find their way. I believed Jacob had found his niche. Christian and Rylan were Jakari's younger brothers, but we all grew up like siblings since my mama and Aunt Chrissy were so close. Mal was our parents' first cousin, but he was still bull riding, so he was in and out.

I went back to my food that was now cold and picked over it a bit before closing the box. Jakari grabbed my hand, and Nesha grabbed the other. No one said anything. We used to do that all the time as kids, because our parents were all in turmoil because of shit either our grandparents did or our fathers. Jakari's dad was a fucking pedophile, and they didn't find out until he was grown and in college.

That shit threw him for a loop. They hated that muthafucka, and I did too for what he'd done to Nesha and her sisters. Then all the bullshit Nesha went through with her dad was a lot.

"Go meet Brix. While your heart may not be ready right now, I still think he's who you need," Nesha said.

"I don't want to feel like I'm using him though. I'm going to meet Nate next weekend, and I don't know what's going to come of that."

"I know. You gon' have a decent time, but all you gon' be thinking about is Brix," Jakari added.

"So now you a prophet?"

"Hell yeah. Anybody that has been paying attention can prophesy that outcome."

I rolled my eyes and was gathering my food when I said, "I'll call him when I leave."

"Call who?" a voice I recognized as Brixton's said.

That was what I got for sitting with my back to the door. I never usually did that, but my mind was far away from here when I first got here. Nesha was sitting there with a silly smile on her face, and Jakari looked just as stupid. I stood from my seat and turned to see him standing there with a bouquet of roses. I bit my bottom lip and closed my eyes as I responded, "You."

It came out as a whisper, but I knew he heard me. When his fingers stroked my cheek, I opened my eyes and stared at him. I could feel the tears building, so I looked away and cleared my throat. "You wanna chill out with me in person instead of by phone?" he asked.

"Yeah. You owe me an apology anyway."

He frowned as I took the flowers from him. "For what?"

"Bestie Jessie, nigga?"

He glanced at Jakari, and they laughed hard as hell. I rolled my eyes and made my way to the kitchen to tell my mama that I would see her later. She was sliding peach cobbler in the oven, and I had to stand still and take in the aroma. "That smells so good."

She turned to me with a smile on her face. "Thank you, baby. I'll bring some home."

I smiled back at her. "I'm about to leave with Brix."

"Is that who bought you those beautiful flowers?"

"Yes, ma'am. Listen, we need to talk about some things. I know you can sense when things aren't quite right with me, and I made a vow to you on Christmas day that I would do better about letting you in. If it's not too late when I get back, can we talk tonight?"

"Of course, baby. If I'm asleep, wake me up."

"I'm not going to wake you up. If it's too late, we can just talk tomorrow morning. Okay?"

"Okay. See you later, and be careful."

"I will."

I walked out of the kitchen to see Lennox and Brixton sitting at the table with Nesha and Jakari. They seemed to be getting acquainted. I stood there and watched until they noticed me. Brixton stood and shook Lennox's hand then made his way to me. "You wanna ride with me, or will you just follow me home?"

"I'll follow you home. You might try to hold me hostage."

"Girl, if you only knew. The thought has crossed my mind a few times since Thursday night. If the Hendersons didn't run so deep around here, I would have done it already."

I chuckled as I playfully pushed him. I took a deep breath, prepared to just relax in his arms and worry about everything else later.

CHAPTER SIX

BRIXTON

When Jakari texted me, saying to come to the diner and rescue Jess from herself, I stopped working and immediately went into the house and showered, then went all the way to Beaumont to get her some flowers. I'd barely made it there before she left, but there was no way I was going to go there empty handed, especially not when I knew she was feeling sensitive and needed me.

I was shocked that Jakari had texted me in the first place. I supposed everyone had witnessed our chemistry Saturday night. I surely thought he'd *been* told her about Bestie Jessie and how I planned to break out the friend zone. I chuckled again at the thought. Sometimes I wished I wouldn't have let her dad punk me into staying away from her, especially since I knew how he was treating her. I was a kid, though, and I was raised to respect my elders.

That nigga wasn't worth the respect he was given. When I left for San Marcos, I left Jess behind and regretted every moment of that shit. No matter how many women I dated or fucked, I knew if I ever came in contact with her again and she was single, I would try my hardest to make her mine.

When I parked in the driveway, I hurriedly got out of my truck to go and help her from her car. While I knew she wouldn't be here long, I wanted to cherish the little time we had before she went out with her cousins. It was already after one in the afternoon. As I opened her door, she leaned over to get her flowers and her food. The skirt she had on had a split that gave me the perfect view of her long ass legs, especially those thick ass thighs. *Shat!*

Jessica was so fucking fine without even trying to be. She was just a damn natural. That honey-colored skin covering her five feet nine inches of perfection was one of my favorite things about her. Her skin tone complemented my chocolate skin tone perfectly. Her dark-colored eyes slanted upward, and her cheekbones were high. When she smiled big, her cheeks turned her eyes into slits that accented her already beautiful face. Her smile could brighten up anyone's day.

I didn't see that split that clearly when she walked, but got damn if I didn't see it now. That shit showed her entire leg. If it were an inch higher, I would catch a glimpse of the ultimate prize. She turned to me, and I took the food from her and grabbed her hand to help her up. She smiled at me as I closed her door then grabbed her hand again.

Words weren't spoken, and I was okay with the silence. It spoke volumes. She was definitely in her feelings, but I knew she just wanted to relax and sort of go with the flow. I knew her well enough to know that her actions didn't necessarily mean there was a change in our status, but it *did* mean there was hope. She wouldn't be this way with me if there wasn't a possibility for more.

After I opened the door, I set her food on the countertop, and she set her flowers right next to it. I pulled her in my arms to hold her, but she had other plans. Her lips met mine, giving me the sweetest kiss I'd ever received from her. Her glossed lips slowly glided against mine until she slid her tongue to mine. The kiss went from sweet to passionate in seconds, and I displayed pure acceptance with that transition.

My hands slid down her back and gripped her ass as I broke the kiss with her lips and made my way to her neck. The moan that left her only propelled me forward, my lips moving to her bare shoulder. "Brix... what about your mother?"

"She ain't here, baby. She's in Beaumont," I said roughly in her ear then bit her lobe, diamond stud and all.

I grabbed her ponytail, pulling her head further back and licked up the front of her neck to her chin and crashed my lips against hers. She lifted her leg to my waist, and I gripped the hell out of it. Feeling her soft skin was fucking me up. Damn, I wanted her so bad, and I could only hope that this shit she incited would be going all the way, because I was nearing the point of no return.

I picked her up and set her on the island right here in the kitchen. Plans of going further into the house had been completely abandoned. After she laid those lips on me, I lost all focus. I pulled away from her to lock the door. I didn't know what time my mama was coming back, and there was no way I would leave the door unlocked for her to just walk in on us like this. When I turned back to Jess, she was staring right at me.

"Brix, I don't know what I want relationship wise. Sexually, I'm always ready, but I can't be thinking with my pussy. That's how people get hurt. Maybe we should—"

I put my fingers on her lips, silencing her. "Stop thinking so much. I wanna tell you something I been wanting to tell you for years."

I pulled away from her, then went to the sink to wash my hands. I hated to break the mood, but I planned to dive in her pussy, and I didn't need any impurities altering anything about her. She was staring at me intently as I made my way back to her. "What have you been wanting to tell me, Brix?"

I licked my lips and slid my hand between her legs, stopping short of her heater. I spread her legs open wider and stood closer to her. After staring at her for a moment, I slid my fingers past her panties and watched her eyelids flutter as her head dropped back some. "Come be my good girl, Jess. I want you to take this dick like a good girl."

Her body temperature seemed to increase suddenly, and her pussy went from just being wet to flooding my fucking fingers and leaking down my hand to my arm. "You been wanting to hear that, baby?" I asked as she moaned.

"Yeeeeessss, Brix. Fuuuuck."

I began stroking her faster, but she pulled my arm away from her, causing my fingers to withdraw. I immediately licked what was rolling down my arm until I got to my fingers, then sucked them into my mouth while she watched. Her taste was just as exquisite as I knew it would be. She hiked her skirt up and pulled her top over her head. Seeing her titties had me painfully erect. She wasn't wearing a bra. When I took my fingers from my mouth, she grabbed my hand and sucked them into hers.

Her hands made their way to the waistband of my jeans, and she unbuckled my belt then unbuttoned my pants. She did that shit fast as hell. I pulled my fingers from her mouth and watched her saliva roll down them. I licked all that shit up before pulling my pants down and whipping my dick out of that confined space he was in. Jess slid from the countertop and went to her knees, pulling my dick into her slick ass mouth.

I moaned immediately. It had been a few months since I'd gotten head, but to have Jessica's lips wrapped around my shit was like a dream come true. I slid my hands to her face as we stared at one another. The frown made its way to my face because she was sucking the fucking life from me. My legs were trembling and getting weak as hell. "Oh fuck, Jess!"

She was leaving spit all over my dick, and it was throbbing like crazy, ready to spew the effects of his fulfilled dreams. I began stroking her mouth as the tears fell from her eyes. Using my thumbs, I wiped them away while I fucked her tonsils up, trying to show her tenderness, even in this moment. "Jess, I'm about to cum, baby."

She tightened her suction and sucked me harder, causing goosebumps to invade my skin. It felt like she was taking my breath, because I could barely catch that shit. My dick spasmed for seconds like it was trying to build up pressure to blow her fucking throat up. The strength of it had my lower back tightening. As it burst through, I yelled, "Fuuuuck!"

Jessica had damn near taken my manhood. She closed her eyes and digested every ounce of excitement I had released. I was weak as fuck! She had my ass stumbling. What made it worse was that she still had a hold on my dick. She was stroking it, milking him for everything he had. She licked the tip, ingesting what came out when she squeezed him then stood. I grabbed her face rough as hell and shoved my tongue down her damn throat. Here I was, thirty-one years old, and that was the best head of my entire life.

I pulled away from her and lifted her back to the island. I sat on the stool in front of her and ripped her panties at the crotch and went right in. She pulled her skirt out of the way and put her hand at the back of my head, pushing me in deeper. "Yeeeeesss, Brix! Fuck!"

Her pussy was so damn wet I couldn't keep up with the output. That shit was running through my beard and down my damn neck, promising to offer it the deep conditioning it needed. I moaned as I indulged in what Jazmine Sullivan described as the best pussy in the world in one of her songs. I lifted my head and said just that. "Fuck, girl. I ain't never had no shit like this. This gotta be the best pussy in the fucking world."

I tapped her enlarged clit with my fingertips and watched the cream leak from her. I went right to it and slurped that shit up. "Brix! Fuck your shit up, baby!" she screamed.

My shit, huh? I submerged my whole fucking face in her shit as I sucked her clit and finger fucked her G-spot. I growled against her shit, and she sprayed that good shit all over me. I couldn't keep going at that point. I had to have her now. My dick was throbbing and begging to be put out of his misery. I stood from the stool and pushed her forward, getting on the island with her, and entered her with haste. My eyes rolled to the back of my head.

I remained still and somehow focused my gaze on Jessica. She was staring at me as the tears fell down her cheeks. I lowered my face to hers and slowly licked her tears. I wanted to digest all the pain and heartache for her. Once I began stroking her, she wrapped her arms around me. "Mmm," I moaned. "Shit, that's my good girl. Drown this muthafucka, Jess. This yo' shit."

Her eyes fluttered shut, and she wrapped her thick ass thighs around me as I stroked her slowly but deeply. "Briiiixx... this shit feel so good. I'm about to cuuuuummm."

"Give it to me, Jess."

When I felt the tremble in her thighs, I knew it was right there without her saying so. I lowered my lips to her nipples and kissed each one then pulled one into my mouth. They were so beautiful. Everything about this woman was beautiful. She was definitely model material. Her pussy clenched me tightly as she spasmed, sinking her point-tipped nails in my back. That shit only turned me on more.

I released her nipple just as she screamed and came, drowning my dick as I requested of her. I pulled out of her and slid from the countertop then scooped her from it and brought her to the recliner I always sat in. Once I sat, she straddled me, sliding down my dick as I reclined it. I bit my bottom lip as I lay back, soaking up everything she had to offer me. "Ride yo' shit, Jess. Give my pussy to me, baby. Say this my shit again."

I gripped her hips as she bounced, staring right into my eyes. Her lips parted, but the words never left her. I began meeting her strokes, jabbing her pussy with punches that were sure to take her out in just a minute. "Tell me this my shit, Jess! Fuck!"

"Brix! Fuck! Fuck it like it's yours!"

"Naw. This shit *is* mine! Now tell me that shit!" I yelled as I began fucking her up from below.

I wrapped my arms around her waist and tore her fucking cervix up until she screamed, "This your pussy, Brix! Fuck! This yo' shiiiit!"

I pulled her nipple into my mouth and sucked it like a newborn as she came all over me. "I'm about to nut. Where you want it, Jess?"

She hesitated, so I said, "You better make a decision quick before I shoot up paradise."

"I'm on the pill, so this will be the best shoot I've ever been a part of."

She brought her lips to mine and sucked the hell out of my top and bottom lips then gave me her tongue. When she pinched both of my nipples, I fired off, letting my seed free. "Ahh, fuck!"

She laid her head on my chest as we both recouped from the most amazing sex I'd ever had. I could only imagine what it would be like in a bed where we wouldn't be as restricted. There was just no way I could make it to the bedroom. Jess lifted her head and stared at me, probably in disbelief like me. We were no longer just friends. She brought her hand to my mouth and traced my lips with her fingertips. Her eyes closed and she said, "We need to clean up before your mom gets here."

"Mm hmm," I responded as I stroked her back.

She kissed my lips, and as she tried to pull away, I slid my tongue into her mouth. She indulged for a moment then pulled back. I released my hold on her and watched her lift from my dick. That nigga was hard all over again, wanting to be back in her rain forest. She stood from the chair and went to the kitchen and gathered her clothes, slipping her top and skirt back on, then got Clorox wipes from the countertop near the sink.

I huffed and stood from the chair and put my clothes on as well, being sure to put her torn panties in my pocket. As she wiped the island, I slid my arms around her from behind. She stilled in my embrace then turned to me. "I'm sorry. I have to go."

"No you don't. Talk to me. You've only been here an hour."

She looked away from me. "Jess, I know this doesn't mean you're giving in to me. I'm patient as fuck when it comes to you. I don't wanna mess shit up, baby. I just want you to be comfortable enough to just be. What we just shared was beautiful."

She took a deep breath and lowered her head. "It was amazing, Brix. Damn. Even better than I imagined."

"Well, please don't leave yet. Let me spot mop this floor, and we'll do whatever you want. I can see you got a nap crawling all over you right now. I'm with that too, baby. Just don't leave."

She smiled slightly. "Okay."

I got the wet jet and mopped in front of the island as she continued wiping the countertop. This was one mess I didn't mind cleaning up after. When we were done, I could hear my mama driving up the driveway. I smiled at her and led her to the recliner. After sitting, I pulled her on top of me and reclined. "Brix, I don't want to give your mom the wrong impression."

"And what impression is that? I wanna be next to you. If we sit on the couch, she's gonna sit in this recliner. Would you be able to handle that sight?"

She chuckled as her face reddened. "Hell naw."

I laughed then pulled her to me and kissed her lips. "It doesn't matter what anybody thinks. We know what this is. Okay?"

She smiled slightly and lay on my shoulder. If only I could convince her that this was where she should be, I'd be doing good.

CHAPTER SEVEN

JESSICA

I'd been questioning things for a while. I supposed I was questioning God. Ever since Decklan started distancing himself in our relationship, I'd been wondering, *where is the love?* I'd even asked Decklan that question in one of our arguments. *Where is the love that you promised me?* It seemed love was avoiding me. He picked a fine time to show that he didn't love me. He waited until I'd fallen for him. I'd let my guard down concerning love and men altogether. My worst fear of being hurt and heartbroken had become a reality.

However, it turned out that I had been with the wrong men, because I clearly felt passion, tenderness, and maybe even love from Brixton. It wasn't like it was too soon because we'd known one another for years. No matter how much time had passed, we were still the same people at our core. Our connection was just as intense as it was back then. I was still somewhat reserved when it came to how much of my inner workings I made him privy to, but I knew that I would eventually share my soul with him.

I needed time to be sure that he was, for certain, the one I was meant for. I felt a connection to Nate too. I'd only been avoiding seeing him because it was so soon after my breakup with Decklan. Here it was, three months later, and I was still trying to get over my heartbreak. It was way too fresh when I first met him. Our phone conversations had been nice, though, despite how short they were.

He was always busy, and so was I, but we talked when we could, which was usually before one of us passed out for the night. Tonight would be different. I would be in his space. He'd offered for me to stay at his house with him, and I was still mulling that over. Thoughts of my experience with Brixton had been on my mind since I'd left Nome a week ago. The way he took care of my body had left me in a haze, wishing that we would have said to hell with Joseph and just been together.

I would have followed his ass to San Marcos and went to school there too. I could have gotten a business degree anywhere. The only reason I stayed closer to home was so I could check on my mama and get there quickly if I needed to. Only Jacob and I knew what was going on in that house, and I was more than sure we didn't know everything.

However, Brix decided to come along at a time when my heart was in turmoil. It was filled with confusion on where to turn after Decklan. I didn't want to trust another man to care for my soul. That shit with Decklan had caught me so off guard. My heart absorbed all the hurt and guilt. I felt the guilt because I blamed myself for picking the wrong man to love. I felt like I should have seen that within him.

Nate had eased my turmoil while I was with him, and I was curious to see if it felt the same way being around him. Either way, I knew I had to be good within before I could be good with anyone else. I thought I was until Brix told me things about Joseph, and Decklan popped up on me at the family party. My vulnerability was back, and I was afraid that sleeping with Brix had been a mistake... a bad decision. I didn't mistakenly fall on his dick. *And what a magnificent dick it is.*

As the car took me to the Toyota Center, I received a text from

Brix. We'd been communicating since I left Nome, mostly by text. I was so busy with my shoot. I ended up doing a second shoot while I was there. It was last minute, but I didn't turn down an easy bag. Modeling had come second nature to me, and I felt like I was the full-figured G.O.A.T. when it came to it. My face was damn near everywhere, and it would only be a matter of time before I exploded. Shylou and Carter were grooming and preparing me for that.

I looked at my phone to see what he wanted to say. *Enjoy the game tonight, baby. I miss you.*

Just from his text, I wanted to tell this man to make a U-turn and head back to Nome. I knew I needed to explore this though. I would always wonder if Nate and I would have worked out if I didn't. I responded to his text. *Thanks, Brix. Miss you too.*

That was the truth. I missed him like crazy. That was the only tough part about traveling so much. I was always alone. When the car came to a stop, I looked up at the stadium. I hadn't been to a professional game in a long time. Nate told me that I would be up top in the box seat. I wasn't really feeling all that. I wanted to be in the stands with the fans, enjoying the game, but whatever.

The driver opened the door for me and helped me from the car. I was here two hours early, but I was sure that was so Nate could see me before the game. When I walked inside, my suspicions were confirmed. Nate was standing there waiting for me. I smiled at him as he looked over my body in this catsuit. I'd worn a duster over it with a belt around it, but it still didn't hide shit. I'd noticed in the mirror before leaving that I could practically see the outline of my pussy in this shit. It was too late to change.

"Hey, Jess. You look good as hell, baby."

"Hey, Nate. You look good too," I responded as I stared up at him.

The man was more than a foot taller than me. He pulled me close, and I wrapped my arms around his waist. I closed my eyes, waiting to feel the sparks I felt the night before Nesha's wedding. They weren't here. I pulled away and smiled at him. He lowered his lips and lightly pecked my lips. *There it is.* My entire body heated up when his lips touched mine. I lifted my hand and rubbed the lipstick from his lips.

"Good luck tonight on your game, Nate."

"Thanks, Jess. I'm glad you're here," he said as he grabbed my hand, leading me further inside. "You're all I've been able to think about since Christmas. You stole my attention and have yet to give it back. That has to mean something, right?"

"I suppose," I said. He wasn't the only man that had my attention, so I surely didn't want to entertain this conversation. "When did you get in town?"

"Yesterday. I chilled out with my mama and grandparents. But something else happened."

"What?"

"I made contact with Noah. He seemed excited to meet me. He's gonna be here tonight."

"Wow, Nate! I'm so happy for you. Were you able to get an idea of just who your father was?"

"Not really. We didn't get to talk long, but he promised that we would have a day to talk soon. Our schedules seem to clash. When he's available, I'm not, and vice versa. Hopefully by the time the season is over, we'll get to hook up. He's been busy in the studio with a couple of his artists, and two of his artists had albums released, one of which was his daughter. So he's been running nonstop."

"I can understand that. So it has to be a big deal that he'll be here tonight."

The excitement was evident in his eyes. "Yeah. It's almost like he's my brother in a way. I've always wanted a big brother."

He chuckled, and the smile that ensued was beautiful. I brought my hand to his cheek and stroked it. He grabbed my hand and kissed it as he stared into my eyes. "You're so beautiful, Jess, even more beautiful than I remember. Damn."

My cheeks heated under his gaze, and he pulled me in for a hug again. I closed my eyes for a moment, soaking in his excitement. I knew that my presence was part of the reason for his mood. He began walking again, my hand still in his as we got stares from people passing us and head nods from other players. When we got to the point where we had to go separate ways, he turned to me and smiled.

"Enjoy the game. Hopefully, you'll be my good luck charm."

I smiled back as he lowered his head to mine. His excitement had me feeling excited too. I was glad that I had made the decision to come. When he kissed me, I decided to give him more than he'd initiated. When I slid my tongue to his, he held me tighter and went deeper too. His kiss was everything I remembered it to be, and that only filled me with even more turmoil. I would have to make a choice. I couldn't have them both.

He pulled away, and I, again, tried to wipe the lipstick from his lips. I pulled his face to mine then leaned to kiss his neck. "Leave that lipstick there. Have a good game, Nate."

He pecked my lips again and backed away from me, backpedaling until he no longer could. I turned and went to the bathroom to freshen my lipstick, then made my way to the box. *Damn.* Nate was everything I remembered him to be. This would be a great night, but the decision on who to choose would affect me a lot more than I anticipated.

THE GAME HAD BEEN AMAZING. Nate had scored twenty-eight points... four were three-pointers. Although he wasn't the star player of the team, he'd significantly contributed to their win tonight. Noah had arrived at halftime, and several had asked him for autographs. He was a star rapper and producer and hall of fame inductee. He was definitely an A-list celebrity. I didn't approach him because I was sure that Nate would introduce us.

Noah stayed inside the box while I drifted out to the hallway.

When my phone rang and I saw my girl Tyeis's number, I answered. "Hello?"

"Bitch! You at the game? I saw yo' ass on TV. How the fuck you made it to the box?"

"Ty, you know how. Nate invited me out."

"Aww shit. So y'all gon' finally go to the next phase of whatever the fuck y'all doing?"

My mind immediately went to Brix. That was most likely a sign. He'd entered my mind more times than I could count tonight. "Not now, Ty. I still don't know what direction I'm gonna go in. I reconnected with someone in my hometown, and it got intense last week."

"Oh shit. You fucked him."

I closed my eyes as I thought about the love Brix had shown me. "Yeah. I just don't know. Maybe I should stay single for right now. I'm so damn conflicted."

"You have to let go of fear, Jess. Who does your heart want?"

"That's the problem. I don't know yet. I get the feels around both of them. I haven't been around Nate long enough yet, though, to truly compare the two of them."

"Well, you should know after tonight then. When do you have another break?"

"Well, I guess I'm on somewhat of a break now. I make an appearance at a club tomorrow night, then I'm off for a week and a half before I leave for California."

"Take me to your hometown. I gotta meet this dude. What's his name?"

"Brixton."

"Damn. That's a sexy ass name. Maybe I can find me a country nigga while I'm out there."

I rolled my eyes. That was where I went wrong. I met Lennox and thought that anyone associated with him was like him... had his morals and values. I was wrong as hell. "I have a couple of single cousins close to your age. They are a little younger, but not by much."

"Girl, as long as they're in their thirties or older, I'm good. I can't be dating nobody closer to my daughter's age."

Tyeis was thirty-eight, but she looked young. I thought she was in her twenties when I met her. Then she told me she had an eighteen-year-old daughter, and I was even more amazed. She was a single mother, doing her best to make her way through life, taking care of her daughter. The modeling thing came up unexpectedly. She was working in human resources for Shylou's businesses when he realized she needed to be one of his faces instead of working behind the scenes.

She told me she hopped on that opportunity so fast. She was giddy to show off her new body. She'd had a bariatric procedure to assist her in losing weight. I wasn't sure which one she had, but she was down nearly one hundred pounds. She looked amazing. Her weight was affecting her health, physical and mental, so she knew she had to do something about it. I was so happy that she had progressed, especially mentally, from where she was prior to her surgery.

"I have two cousins, Decaurey and Jakari."

"Oh shit. Don't tell me they're twins."

"No. Technically, Decaurey is my uncle's stepson, but we claim him as our cousin. He would probably be offended if he even heard this explanation. Jakari is my first cousin. Jakari is thirty, about to be thirty-one, and I think Decaurey is thirty-two or so. They both are businessmen. Jakari is running our family business with our uncle, and Decaurey owns his own cement company. Decaurey likes older women too. He was dating a woman like twenty years older than him."

"Well, it seems I have the pick of the litter then. I'll be in H-Town Saturday morning and ready to hit the road with you. Is there a hotel close?"

I chuckled. "Girl, naw. I'm surprised ain't nobody in my family built one. But shit, Nome ain't no fucking tourist attraction. Most people that visit are there to see family. You can probably stay at my parents' house with me. I'll check to make sure it's okay, although I'm sure it is since my dad knows you."

Tyeis knew that my biological dad was deceased and that Carter was my stepfather. However, she had no clue about my past with Joseph. "Okay, boo. Let me know. In the meantime, I'll keep Decaurey on my mind, because he seems to be more my speed. What happened to the older woman he was dating?"

I noticed Nate heading my way, so I said, "I'll let him cue you in on that. I have to go, boo. I'll call you tomorrow."

"Okay. Have fun."

I ended the call just as Nate wrapped his arms around me and picked me up. When he spun me around, I laughed loudly. After lowering me to my feet, he said, "You were definitely my good luck charm."

"You had an amazing game. Congratulations."

He bit his bottom lip then brought his lips to mine and kissed me tenderly. My eyes fluttered shut, and when he pulled away, I opened them slowly to see his gorgeous smile. I couldn't help but smile back whenever he smiled at me. He grabbed my hand and led me back inside the box to where Noah was.

They slapped hands and hugged like they'd known one another forever. After they separated, Noah's eyes landed on me. "This your lady? Why didn't you say anything to me?"

"Jess is my friend. I'm working on getting her to be my lady though."

Nate kissed the side of my head. "I didn't want to bother you. Enough people were doing that. I'm Jessica. Nice to meet you."

"Nice to meet you too." He turned his attention back to Nate and said, "Damn. You look even taller in person. David would have been so proud, man."

We all sat in chairs as they talked. Noah only had a few more minutes to spare, and they talked about David for every second of that time while I looked on in excitement. Seeing them connect and Nate get familiar with who his dad was as a person was heartwarming. When Noah told him of David's dad still being in Houston and taking him to meet him on his next trip to Houston, Nate looked like he wanted to explode inside.

What took the cake though was Noah telling Nate that he reminded him so much of David. I hated this for him. The way Noah described David, it seemed he would have been an amazing dad to Nate. The fact that his mother denied him that privilege irritated me. He and Noah talked for another few minutes, then we stood to leave.

"Ms. Jessica, it was nice meeting you. For the record, I know you're a model. I've seen you around. Be looking for a call, shorty."

My eyebrows lifted in shock. I didn't know entertainers were looking for big girls these days. These rappers always wanted their models to be slim in the waist with big, fake ass titties and BBLs and shit. He chuckled at my reaction then asked, "Have you seen my wife? Don't be surprised. She doesn't want to be in every video, so I need somebody close to her body type. I think TAZ will appreciate my efforts."

I smiled and said, "I appreciate that. I'll be waiting."

I was way too excited. Shylou was gonna be excited as hell, and I was gonna text him as soon as we were out of Noah's presence. Carter wasn't as involved in hip hop culture. He was more into R&B and jazz, but I knew he liked Noah. He wore his R&B album out. Nate and Noah hugged one another again and promised to see each other again soon. When he left out with his bodyguards, Nate dropped to the chair and brought his hands to his face.

I sat next to him and pulled one of his hands from his face. When I saw how red his face was, I gently stroked his cheek for a moment. His emotions were on the verge of spilling over. I pulled my hand away from his cheek and placed it on top of our joined hands, caressing his hand between mine as he stared at me.

"Jess, hearing how much of a father David was to Noah angers me. I could have had that same thing. Knowing that my mother denied me of that hurts. I told her I forgave her for that, but this shit is hard. It's hard not to feel animosity toward her after hearing about all the times he was there for a man he called his son, when he had a son he didn't know about."

I lowered my head. It seemed we had similar issues. Deciding to share, I said, "I blamed my mother for a long time for what I went through with my biological father. He was abusive, mostly verbally. My mother knew what was going on because he was abusive to her too. While she tried to build me up to help me forget about the insults he hurled my way, I felt like she didn't protect me from him. She should have left him long before it even got to that point."

Nate began rubbing my hands now as I continued. "I came to the realization that she did her best and what she thought was best at the time. She made a bad decision by staying, and it could have destroyed me, but it didn't. It shaped me into who I am now. There's nothing she can do about it now but apologize, and she's done that more times than I can count. It's in the past. Your mother made a bad decision by keeping you away from your father. But what can she do about it now?"

He closed his eyes for a moment. While I was trying to help him cope, I'd actually helped myself. That situation with Brix angered me, but what could anyone do about it now? Not a damn thing. I was only working myself up all over again about Joseph being a bullshit ass nigga. I knew that was what he was before Uncle WJ took his pathetic ass out of here and before I moved to Houston. Nothing he did should surprise me or affect me to the point where it took control of my emotions.

Nate took a deep breath and said, "You're right, baby. Let's get out of here."

He helped me from my seat and draped his arm over my shoulder as we left the room to head to his car. As we walked down the long hallway, he asked, "Was your mother defending her actions at first?"

"No. She explained why she made the decisions she did. She was disgusted with herself and the mistakes she'd made. I believed her explanation was more for herself than for me. Listening to her talk freed me from the anger in my heart. We all handle situations differently. My mama had the feistiness beat out of her, and she became a different person after that. She was way too submissive and secretive, because she didn't want her brothers to get in trouble for whatever they would have done to Joseph had they found out."

"My mother got angry that I was questioning her. All she kept saying was that David was a ho and that there was no way he would have been ready to take care of a child. Listening to how he took care of a child that wasn't his contradicts everything she's told me about him."

I squeezed his hand, forcing him to stop walking. When he turned to me, I said, "People can be different with different people. Chances are that David wasn't the same person with your mother as he was with Noah and his mother. I'm more than sure he wasn't perfect, and maybe he hurt your mother more than what she's admitting. From what Noah said, he never remarried, and none of the women he messed around with were at his bedside when he died. Maybe he left a trail of broken hearts in his wake. Unfortunately, that could have affected his ability to be a good father because your mother didn't want to be reminded of how he treated her."

"How did you become so wise?" he asked as he stroked my cheek.

"Hmph," I voiced as I looked away. I turned back to him and said, "Jenahra Henderson Wothyla… my mother. Despite her mistakes in life, she imparted her wisdom in me."

He kissed my hand then nodded. We continued down the hallway, and his guards opened the door for us and escorted us to the car. When we got in, Nate pulled me to his lap, causing me to straddle him, then laid his forehead on my shoulder. I brought my hand to the back of his head and let him be as he wrapped his arms around my waist.

The anger had dissipated, but I could still feel his pain. I stroked the back of his head, allowing him a moment to pull himself together. The moment he did, he kissed the side of my head and said in my ear, "I'm sorry. Thank you for your encouraging words, Jess."

"You don't have to thank me. This situation has helped me too. So, thank *you*."

His hands slid to the small of my back as he sat back in his seat and lifted his head to stare into my eyes. No words were spoken, but the intensity of the silence was overwhelming. When the tears fell down my cheeks, he gently wiped them away, and I wiped away the couple that had fallen down his cheeks as well. At this moment, we were kindred spirits and needed one another tonight more than we could have ever imagined.

CHAPTER EIGHT

BRIXTON

I texted Jess first thing Friday morning and went on with my day. I didn't hear from her until she was about to head to a club that night. Patience wasn't my strongest virtue, but I normally could wait for what I knew would be worth it. Waiting on Jess was proving to be hard as hell. I believed knowing where she was made it more difficult. Had she been at work or in Nome, it wouldn't have been as hard. Knowing she was with Nate, someone she had feelings for, made things tense for me.

He was probably holding and kissing her the way I had just a little over a week ago. I wasn't a jealous nigga, but the thought of that shit wasn't doing good things for me. Jessica's heart belonged to me. While she may have been confused about that shit, I could see it clearly. She'd gotten way too angry and hurt about what her dad did that kept us from being together. If she didn't want me, that shouldn't have upset her as much as it did.

I hadn't texted her this morning because I assumed she probably got home late last night from the club. My entire mind was focused on her and what she could be doing, telling me to send a message anyway and that she would see it when she woke up. One thing I had never done was chase someone who didn't seem to be on the same wave as me. While I knew Jessica was feeling me, I also knew she needed time.

As I attached the new gate I'd bought on the fence, a truck turned in my driveway. I wasn't sure who it could be, because the only person that had just shown up here was Kenny Henderson. Ever since that day he'd helped me with the fence, he'd been checking in to see if I needed any more help. He was the one who suggested I got a new gate for this side of the fence.

When the white man got out of the truck, I stood and stared, waiting for him to get closer so I could see what he wanted. "Hello! Are you Mr. Phillip Lewis?"

"No. He's deceased."

"Oh. I apologize. So who assumes ownership of this property?"

"My mother, Helen Lewis."

"Is she here?"

I had a feeling this was regarding those muthafuckas that had been bothering me about my father owing them money. They'd never brought any proof of that shit, and I refused to pay them just on their word. "Follow me."

Mama was in the kitchen, preparing lunch. She'd promised to make us patty melts, and I couldn't wait to sink my teeth into one. When we got to the back door, I turned to him and said, "Wait here."

I closed the door and locked it as my mama turned to look at me. She frowned slightly. "What's going on?"

"There's a man outside that is asking for the property owner. What's going on that you haven't told me?"

She swallowed hard then walked toward the door without responding to me. This shit was on my nerves. I hated secrets, especially ones that would affect me in some way. I'd been putting in all this fucking work on this property for months, and it seemed somebody else may have had a legal right to it. That was what I was assuming from this situation. I hadn't even heard what was going on, but just her silence was saying it all. It was something that was going to piss me all the way off.

She opened the door and invited the man inside. He thanked her for her hospitality then got to the point. "I didn't realize that your name was on these documents as well. This is a promissory note you and your husband signed, basically putting the house up as collateral for a loan you took out with Mr. Jeffcoat in the amount of forty grand."

My eyes widened. *Forty fucking thousand dollars!* That shit pissed me off beyond belief. They could have asked me for that money. I didn't have forty grand I could just give to them, but I could have taken out a loan at the bank. I could have called my sister, Stacy, to see if she could put in some money to help. There were so many other options they could have taken besides borrowing money from some old white man that would take their fucking property.

I was steaming as the man showed her the documents. "We wanted to give you an opportunity to pay it off, before taking legal action. This document gives you thirty days to pay the amount in full before he submits paperwork to obtain this house and all twenty acres."

I grabbed my keys and walked outside. I wasn't going to leave until he left, but I couldn't take hearing another word. I was too pissed. I'd put in over ten grand worth of work into this place, only for someone else to be able to stake claim to it. This was some bullshit! As I sat there waiting for him to come out of the house, I got a text message from Jessica. It was almost eleven o'clock. I guess she'd really slept in.

I opened her message. *Hey, Brix. I'm back! I'll be at the diner around noon. I hope to see you there.*

That text sounded way too friendly. With the way I was feeling right now, I didn't know if I even wanted to be around her. I could snap on anybody. I briefly closed my eyes and took a deep breath. I sent a response in the affirmative anyway. *Okay. See you there.*

When I saw that man coming out of the house and my mama

standing in the door, watching him leave, I just stared at her. She let me spend all that money, knowing the house and property could be taken at any moment. I could still try to take out a loan, but that shit should have been told to me when I first got here. The gym account had plenty money in it, but that was for operational purposes. I didn't like touching that money if it wasn't for business expenses.

Because of all the money I'd spent, I was down to twenty grand in my personal account. I was so damn mad smoke had to be coming out of my ears. It was best I left to cool off. Otherwise, I'd probably curse my mama out. Had she told me, I could have been making payments on it and not have to come off all that money at once.

Once the man drove off, I backed out of the driveway as well, not bothering to go take a shower. I went straight to Jasper's Liquor and got me a bottle of Jack Daniels and sat in the parking lot of the diner, waiting for Jessica to arrive. I took a swig as my phone rang. It was my mama. I couldn't answer that shit right now. That was why I left. If I was able to talk like I had some sense right now, I would have just stayed there and talked.

After taking a second swig from the bottle, I saw Jessica and another lady getting out of her car. A couple of other cars pulled up on either side of her. I recognized her cousins, Nesha and Jakari. I wasn't sure who the other man was that had gotten out of the other car. I took a deep breath, trying to calm down. Nobody in that restaurant deserved my attitude. I took one more swig, then screwed the bottle closed and got out.

When I made my way inside, I noticed they'd all gone to a far corner of the diner and were talking and laughing loudly. I didn't make my way over immediately. I wasn't that friendly around total strangers. Being that I wasn't in a good mood, it wouldn't be a good idea for me to even chill with them right now.

I went to the counter and ordered a piece of stuffed fried chicken. Today they had been stuffed with macaroni and cheese and greens. I couldn't pass that up. I went to the fountain and got me a Root Beer cream soda. As I got a lid, I saw Jessica heading my way with a huge smile on her face. "Brix! Hey!"

"What's up?" I asked.

Her smile faded as she asked, "You okay?"

"Naw, not really. Something came up, so I won't be able to stay."

"Something like what? You wanna talk about it?" She glanced back at her people then back at me. "We can get a different table."

"Naw. Enjoy your people. I'll talk to you later, okay?"

She grabbed my hand before I could grab my drink from the counter and pulled me to her, but I pulled back immediately. "I didn't take a shower, and I've been working, Jess. We'll talk later."

I pulled my hand away from hers and walked out of the diner without waiting for her response. My nerves were too on edge for me to be there right now. Had it only been her, I would have stayed. I could see the disappointment in her eyes, and I felt bad about that shit. As much as I missed her last week, I couldn't even enjoy being in her presence. That alone was crazy as fuck.

When I got to my vehicle, I set my container of chicken on the passenger seat and put my drink in the cup holder then rested my head on the steering wheel for a second. I knew I would have to take a trip to Beaumont tomorrow to try to get a loan. I would probably fare out better going through my bank in Austin. I could fill out the paperwork online. I just didn't know exactly *how* I would fare out.

The gym wasn't doing as well as it had been. I was taking a hit financially by being out here spending all this money. My dad didn't have life insurance, so my sister and I had to pay for his funeral. My mama couldn't fathom cremating him, although that would have been cheaper. Stacy and I spent over ten grand, a little over five a piece, on his services. I just didn't know what I would do if I didn't get approved. We would lose the farm.

I lifted my head and noticed Jessica standing outside watching me. She began walking toward my truck as I stared at her, wishing she would have just stayed inside. I lowered my window to see what she had to say. When she got to me, she brought her hand to my cheek. "I want to take you to dinner later. Just me and you."

"I don't know. I have a lot of shit on my plate."

"Brix, are you trying to create distance between us? Did I do something?"

"No. I just... I'm just fucked up by something I just found out. I promise I'll call you later and let you know about dinner. Okay?"

She stepped up on the running board of my truck and pressed her lips against mine, then stepped down and walked away without a look back. I didn't know how to tell her what was going on without making it seem like I was asking for money. I didn't want her to think she had to help me. As a man, it was my job to take care of things. I planned to do that... somehow.

"I'M SORRY."

"Mama, you know what this could mean?"

She lowered her head. After I left the diner, I drove to Beaumont and just rode around, trying to clear my head so I could come back here and talk to my mama. When I got home, it was close to three. I went straight to the shower, just in case I decided to join Jessica for dinner. After getting out, I joined my mother in the front room, sat on the couch, and just stared at her for a while before she finally apologized.

She fidgeted, not really wanting to answer my question. She knew exactly what could happen. Instead of letting her off easy with the questioning, I decided to give her the harsh reality. "It means the Jeffcoats will own this place, and you'll either have to move to Austin with me or to New York with Stacy. You will no longer have a place to live. What I don't understand is why y'all borrowed so much money from him in the first place."

"Your grandparents were in over their heads. Production was

slow. As the Hendersons expanded, it took business away from them. This farm was no competition. Your grandfather literally went broke trying to pay the bank back money he'd borrowed. When he died, the money from his life insurance was used to pay them off so they wouldn't take the property. That left no money to operate with. Our credit wasn't good enough to get a loan with the bank, and we didn't want to lose the land. Mr. Jeffcoat was nice enough to let us borrow the money."

"Why didn't y'all say anything? Me and Stacy could have helped y'all! After Dad died, you could have said something so we could have been paying him! I've been here four months, spending money, fixing fence that I could have been using to pay him! So not only did y'all not pay him, but I'm out of over ten grand, if I can't get a loan to pay these people back! Honestly, I don't want to take out a loan, because I may not be able to pay the shit back. You see the position I'm in? Why didn't you say anything?" I yelled.

She shrugged her shoulders nonchalantly, and that pissed me off even more. I'd done all that driving to calm down for nothing, because I was fuming all over again. What it all boiled down to was that they weren't good businessmen. They didn't manage money well. They bought unnecessary shit before taking care of their responsibilities, and that shit irritated the fuck out of me as a kid. We were in the financial predicament we were in because of their ridiculous spending habits.

My mama liked to shop, and it was nothing for her to go to the store and buy shit she didn't need instead of using that money to say... pay the fucking light bill. There were a couple of times that I could remember where our lights had gotten turned off. The shit was embarrassing. Jessica had wanted to come over one time when the lights were off, and I had to lie to her and say that we weren't going to be home.

My dad wasn't any better. He spent all kinds of money on farm equipment he could have rented for the time being. That nigga bought an excavator to clear out some of the land. He only used the shit twice in the five years he had it. Had he used the tractor to just keep the fields mowed, he wouldn't have even needed an excavator. I was gonna have to start slapping for sale signs on shit or take it to the auction.

The auction was a good idea. Tomorrow, I would start loading shit up on that long ass trailer he had that he didn't use either. In the meantime, I needed to get out of here. I stood from my seat and headed to my room to get dressed. I texted Jessica. *I'm sorry about earlier. Where do you want to go for dinner?*

I pulled a maroon, button-down, long-sleeved shirt from the closet, some blue slacks, and brown dress shoes. If she didn't have somewhere in mind, I wanted to take her somewhere nice. Staring at the clothes I'd laid on the bed, I decided to wait for her text before getting dressed. There would be no sense in getting that dressed up if she had other plans. I sat on the bed and played a game on my phone until she responded.

Okay. You don't have to go if you don't want to, Brix. You seem like you want to be alone. I'll be here for a week or so.

I slid my hand down my face and responded immediately. *I want to spend time with you, Jess. I needed to be alone earlier. I'm cool now.*

She didn't respond right away. She was probably having fun with her people. I could have been there with them had it not been for this bullshit my family had us in. I grabbed my clothes from the bed and hung them back up. I had a feeling that she was gonna treat me like I did her earlier. Jess was petty like that. I should have communicated better. I didn't know what I could have said to clue her in, but I should have said something more.

After ten minutes had passed without a response from her, I lay in bed and stared at the ceiling, taking inventory in my mind about everything I could sell. I'd sell every piece of equipment around here if I had to. I could only imagine what the property and school taxes looked like. If they weren't paying Mr. Jeffcoat, I was sure they weren't paying the taxes either. That would be another issue I would have to deal with.

I brought my hands to my face and prayed for strength and answers. I didn't know if I should just chalk this shit up as a loss or fight for it. The Hendersons practically owned Nome. There was no way I could make money here unless they bought cattle and shit from me. They didn't need me. I wasn't a professional with the cattle like they were. I was certain their herd of cattle were much healthier than ours. We only had a hundred head of cattle anyway. They had thousands.

I hated that this shit was controlling my thoughts. My mind was consumed with how I could save this place, but it was in my nature. I was a problem solver. When my phone rang, I was hoping it was Jessica, but it was only Jeffrey, the manager of my gym in Austin. "Hey, Jeff. What's up?"

"What's up, Mr. Lewis? How are things in the country?"

"Stressful as hell. What about out there?"

"We've only had two customers today."

I closed my eyes and bit my bottom lip. "When do you think I should face the inevitable?"

He took in a deep breath and released it. He'd been an employee of mine since I opened the doors six years ago. There was a time when we were busting at the seams. When they opened a Castle Hill Fitness two years ago less than a mile away from us, it killed us. "I think you should face the music now while you're still above water. Don't go broke trying to preserve your pride. Reinvent yourself. You're a businessman. You can change this facility into something else or offer something they don't."

He had a point. However, I'd have to sink my resources out here in Nome, because I knew my mama wouldn't want to move. She'd be homeless in Nome before she lived in Austin or New York. "Okay. Let me think on it. I'll send an email this weekend to all the employees."

I ended the call and yelled, "Fuck!"

Everything seemed to be falling apart around me, and I didn't know how I would come out of this situation. I could only hope Jessica would text back now. I needed to be distracted now more than ever.

CHAPTER NINE

JESSICA

Brixton had me in my feelings big time. I was so excited to get to him I'd rushed Tyeis and fussed about her taking so long all the way to Nome. When he didn't want to spend time with me, I was so disappointed. However, as I watched him leave, I could tell that something was seriously wrong in his world. I wanted him to talk to me, but he had shut me out.

I supposed I wanted the benefits of being his without actually being his. I'd spent the night with Nate Thursday night and didn't talk to Brix at all. Nate and I were intimate, but we didn't have sex. We were both in our feelings about our parents. We talked for hours. We'd held each other all night and kissed some, but he never insinuated he wanted more than that, and neither did I. I still enjoyed being in his company and feeling his embrace.

I was glad that we didn't have sex, because it was too soon after Brix. I needed to marinate in the afterglow his sex gave me. We had an intense sexual chemistry that I wasn't ready to replace with another's. I wanted to just marinate in the love I felt from him, only to get back and feel the opposite. I understood though, because I did the same damn thing. I held stuff in all the time. He'd just been different from me though. He was way more expressive than I was, so his behavior caught me off guard.

"Man, you quiet as hell. You still thinking about Brix?" Jakari asked as he walked in my mama's house.

"Yeah."

Tyeis had gone to the room to take a nap. We'd made plans to turn up with Decaurey, Nesha, and Jakari tonight. I'd hoped Brix would come after we had dinner, but I didn't know if I would even see him again today. I kind of wanted to let him be. He'd sent a text saying he was cool and ready to be near me, but I needed him to make sure. I didn't want to feel like I did at the diner again. I was somewhat embarrassed too.

I'd gassed his ass up to Tyeis about how perfect he was. I'd even told her that I thought he loved me and how he worshiped my body like it was the most beautiful thing he'd ever seen. Then when he got to the diner, I'd hopped up from the table in the middle of conversation to greet him. I expected him to pull me in his arms and kiss me long on the lips. When he barely wanted to touch me, my heart was crushed. Then I had to go back to the table with my heart on my sleeve.

I just knew Ty was gonna clown me, but she could clearly see the hurt on my face. She only rubbed my back and went back to running her mouth with Jakari. They behaved like they were long lost friends. They were interacting more than I was, even before Brix showed up.

"Jess, don't tell him I told you, but Uncle WJ and I were talking about him a little while ago. His dad left him a shit load of debt, and I think he just found out about it today. They owe Mr. Jeffcoat like forty grand, and he done already spent quite a bit of money fixing up the place. They are in jeopardy of losing the property if he doesn't come up with the money in thirty days."

I stared at Jakari in disbelief. "Are you serious? What is he gonna do?"

"I don't know. Uncle WJ called a meeting at six with the siblings, Aunt Chas, Philly, Nesha, and me. He wants to rescue him without taking him over. I don't know how Brix will sustain himself after that though. There are ten years' worth of back taxes on the place. That puts him over a hundred grand in debt. It's not that we don't have the money to bail him out, but there's no sense in doing it if he's gonna fall behind again."

"Well, he has a gym in Austin. And if he's selling cattle and whatnot, shouldn't he be okay?"

Jakari shrugged his shoulders. "I don't know. Philly is checking into his background and financials as we speak so he can have something to present later."

My heart sank at the news. No wonder Brix was so downtrodden earlier. I grabbed my phone and texted him. *We can still go to dinner at about six... just me and you. Wherever you wanna go. If you want, you can come hang out with us after dinner also. I'd love for you to meet my friend, Tyeis.*

"You can't say anything to him about it, Jess. You gon' have to tame that mouth."

"Shut up, fool. I know I can't say anything about it. It would kill him if he knew everyone knew. How did y'all find out?"

"Uncle WJ saw Mr. Jeffcoat's brother leaving their house earlier today on his way to Aunt Tiff's. He stopped him to ask what he was doing there. He told him he'd forgotten to leave a copy of the documents he'd brought by this morning for Ms. Lewis to sign."

"Brix is extremely smart. There's no way he knew about this. That was why he was so upset earlier. I may need to spend the rest of the evening with him and put off going out until later in the week."

A text came through. *I thought you were ghosting me. The time is fine. I'm not sure if I'll want to go out later though. You cool with Pappadeaux?*

Yeah. That's fine. Can I pick you up?

Naw. I'll pick you up, baby.

I took a deep breath. He gave me a term of endearment, and that put my nerves at ease somewhat. I brought my phone to my chest, feeling his pain through every word. "Jess, chill out. You gon' do something to make him think you know. Don't be tryna pay for dinner and shit."

"First of all, nigga, before I even knew about this shit, I asked could I take him to dinner. That means I'm paying, right?"

"Whatever, Jess. He's sensitive to that shit right now, so chill out, or you gon' fuck up."

I rolled my eyes and huffed, knowing that he was probably right. "Fine. I need to go get dressed before he gets here."

"Yeah, because you go through a fucking metamorphosis when you getting dressed sometimes."

"Jakari, shut the fuck up!" I screamed then laughed.

He could irritate the hell out of me at times. He laughed and left as I headed upstairs to shower and get ready for my dinner date. Since we were going to Pappadeaux, I would have to get snazzy. I was glad I brought my blue bodycon dress along. Brix's favorite color was blue, and I planned to work the shit out of it too.

Before I could get in the shower, I heard my mama call out my name. I checked the time, knowing Brix would probably be here in an hour or so. So I yelled, "Come meet me in the bathroom upstairs!"

I started the shower and got clean undergarments from my luggage. I let Tyeis sleep in my bedroom this trip, and I could hear my mama open my bedroom door and close it back. When she found me in the guestroom, she had a slight frown on her face. "Hey, baby. I was so happy to see you earlier, but we were so busy I couldn't stop to hug you."

She hugged me tightly and kissed my cheek. "How was the drive?"

"It was good. Ma, I've been needing to talk to you."

"I know. The last time you were here, I could see it and sense it, but I wanted to let you come to me in your time."

"Come to the bathroom with me. Brix is picking me up in an hour. We can talk while I'm in the shower."

"You sure? We can always talk later, baby."

"I'm sure. We used to talk this way all the time, because it was the only time Joseph wouldn't barge in on us."

She lowered her head and nodded. Whenever I brought up Joseph's name, her reaction was the same. She knew dealing with the aftermath of his abuse had been tough. I got undressed and grabbed a face towel then got in the shower. I let the water soak my face then I wiped it with the towel. "Mama, Brix told me that Joseph forbade him to pursue me."

"What?"

"Brix wanted me to be his in high school, but Joseph threatened to kill him if he pursued me. I think Brix loves me, Mama. He hasn't said so, but I can feel it. Joseph's actions changed my life. I was really feeling Brix back then. What if we would have gotten together and got married? We could have an entire family by now."

"Wow, baby. But listen. There's nothing we can do about it now but to live our lives on our terms. What's meant to be will be. You and Brix have reconnected, and it's not too late to have everything you just talked about. Maybe you needed to go through the dating scene and heartbreak so you would be ready for him. We don't know why God allows some things or allows us to make bad decisions, but we definitely can't question His motives."

"You're right. I came to that conclusion when I talked to Nate after the game Thursday night. He was hurt about not knowing his dad after talking to Noah that night. Noah, the rapper, came to his game. He talked to him about what kind of man his dad was, and it caused Nate to be angry that his mother never apologized about keeping him from his father. He said she's only given him excuses of why she kept him away and kept David in the dark."

"That's tough. He needs to have a serious talk with her."

"He said he would. I told him that she only knew David as the womanizing man that he was. She had no clue what kind of father he would be."

"That's true. I'm glad the two of you were able to talk things through. Did you get angry at me when you found out about Joseph?"

Apparently, I hesitated too long, because she started speaking again before I could respond. "It's okay if you did. I understand totally why that would be your first reaction. What I can respect is that you worked it out and tried to see it for what it was without attacking me about it."

"Mama, I love you so much. I try not to think that way anymore, but when something is revealed about him or what he did to make us miserable, it knocks me back a step. I've learned that when it comes to him and his actions, to think things through. No one made Joseph do the shit he did. He's the one that deserves my anger, but he isn't even here to see it."

"He definitely saw it, Jess. Whenever you came to town and stayed with Tiffany, I got beat for it. He said I was influencing you to be the ho I once was."

I peeked around the shower curtain to look at her. She had never told me that. She swiped tears from her cheek as she said, "I was so happy you got out of the house when you did. He was only going to get worse. He was talking about arranging your marriage and everything. If you wouldn't have been looking to leave, I would have gotten you out of here. There is nothing worse than being with a man that you don't love. I hadn't loved Joseph since you were a baby... hence my affair with Carter."

"I'm so sorry, Mama."

"You don't ever have to apologize. You have become more than I ever imagined. I'm so happy about the woman you became despite the bullshit. I know you hold so much inside. You get that honest, but whenever you choose to settle down again, whether that's with Brix or Nate, be open with them and let them know how you feel about *everything*. Don't hold shit back if you don't like something, and definitely don't settle."

She looked down at her phone as I got out of the shower and grabbed a towel to dry off with. "We have a business meeting in thirty minutes."

"Yeah, Jakari told me."

"Did he say what it was about?"

"He did, but he swore me to secrecy. You'll find out in a little bit. I'm trying to forget that I even know."

"That bad?"

"Not for us, but for someone else."

Her eyes softened, and I could see that she'd figured out it had something to do with Brix. *Why else would Jakari have told me? Duh, Jess.* I might as well had just told her. She stood from the toilet seat and said, "Well, I'm gonna go eat something right quick and let you get dressed. Was there anything else you wanted to say to me, baby?"

She lifted her hand to my cheek, and I leaned against it and closed my eyes. Despite everything, Jenahra Wothyla was my hero. I was a strong woman because of her. "No, ma'am. Just that I love you."

"I love you too, baby. Enjoy your date."

"I will."

When she left out, I went to the bedroom to put on my undergarments. She reappeared in the room though. "I forgot to ask. Why are you in here and not in your bedroom?"

I took a deep breath. "I get anxiety. I feel like I'm suffocating in there."

I didn't have to say another word. She knew exactly why. The tears sprang from her eyes. "I should have remodeled your room too. I didn't think you were as affected as I was. That was so stupid. I'm so sorry, Jess. When y'all head back to Houston, I'll get someone to work on it."

I gave her a slight smile. "It's okay. I should have said something when you were remodeling years ago. Thanks, Mama."

I went to her and hugged her, although I was naked as the day I was born. I was always comfortable around her while I was naked, because Joseph stayed his ass in our business unless I was naked.

He'd walked in on me one time because his ass didn't believe in knocking on a door in his house. I'd developed at a young age, so he got an eyeful and had the nerve to curse at us like it was somehow our fault.

After that, we figured out how to communicate without him being in our business. We either waited until he wasn't home, or we talked while I was taking a shower. She kissed my cheek and said, "Hurry and get ready so you won't keep Brix waiting."

"Jenahra!"

I lowered my head and chuckled as my mama rolled her eyes. Uncle Storm was downstairs yelling. That was what she got for letting him use the diner as his headquarters. I was trying to figure out what the hell he needed a headquarters for. He was so damn extra. I hurriedly went to the bathroom and did my makeup, being sure it was flawless, and made sure my ponytail still looked fresh, then put on my dress, shoes, and switched purses.

When I made my way down, Uncle Storm was still here, pacing in the family room. "Storm, calm down. They are at that age now."

He frowned hard. "They are sixteen! That is not old enough to be dating a college freshman. That boy gon' get fucked up! Dead man walking. He getting one warning. He don't take heed, that's his ass."

"What's going on?" I asked.

"Baby, you look beautiful!"

"Thanks, Mama."

"Noni is texting this guy in college! I'm tryna figure out how the fuck they even meet! She don't hardly go nowhere."

"Have you asked her?"

"No. She's with Aspen in Houston. Oh, but wait until they get back. I'm gon' be all in her shit! She must've forgotten I can look at all their contacts. When I called that nigga, he had the nerve to chuckle. I bet he wasn't chuckling when he heard me loading my gun. I shot that shit while he was on the phone. Pussy ass got quiet as hell too."

"How old is he, Unc?"

"Nineteen! My girls are virgins, and they gon' stay that way! They can't date until they get married. Period!"

I frowned as I repeated what he said in my mind. "What?"

"You heard me right! That means their asses are mine. They'll never date. Fuck they think this is." He slid his hand down his face and huffed. "Come on, Jenahra, so we can get to the meeting." Turning his attention to me, he said, "You look good. It's too late to tell *you* to stay wholesome."

I rolled my eyes and pushed his shoulder. "That's why yo' daughter dating a grown ass nigga."

That shit wiped the smile right off his face as I laughed. "A'ight, Jess! Play with something safe. That shit ain't it!" he said as he pointed at me.

That only made me laugh more. When the doorbell rang, I knew my ride was here. I went to it and opened the door for Brix. *Damn!* If he didn't look good, my name wasn't Jessica. We were damn near matching. We wore the same blue. Had I known, I would've brought my maroon shoes and maroon clutch to match his shirt. *Shit!* "Damn, Brix. You look amazing."

"I was about to say the same thing about you. Fuck. Who you tryna impress? I was impressed seeing you in your overalls and a ponytail in tenth grade when you had to go work with your grandfather after school."

I giggled as he extended the roses in his hand. I invited him inside then kissed his lips. I left his side to go put my flowers in water, but I still heard him say, "Hey, Mrs. Jenahra and Mr. Henderson."

"Hey, Brix. How are you?"

"I'm good."

When I came back, Uncle Storm was just staring at Brix. Finally, he said, "Be good to her. She don't deserve no bullshit."

"You got my word on that."

Uncle Storm leaned over and kissed my cheek. "Have a good time, Ace."

"Thanks. I will."

Brix grabbed my hand and escorted me out of the house to his truck. When we got to the door and he opened it, he lifted me in his arms to put me in the seat. "I didn't want you to mess up your heels on the running board. I didn't realize they were dirty. We'll go to the car wash before we get to the restaurant."

I nodded at him then he closed my door. Although he was being a little looser, I could tell something was bothering him. I just hoped he would choose to talk to me about it so I didn't have to keep pretending I didn't know.

CHAPTER TEN

BRIXTON

The ride to Beaumont was somewhat quiet. I was in my head big time, and I believed she was trying to figure out what my issues were. I knew I had to tell her something so she didn't think I was pushing her away. When we got to the carwash and I put the truck in neutral, I grabbed her hand. "I can't get over how beautiful you look."

"Thank you, Brix. You look very handsome."

I brought her hand to my lips and kissed it as the different color foam coated the windshield. "I know you're wondering what was going on earlier, and frankly, I'm surprised you haven't asked yet."

"I wanted to give you time. Had we gone through dinner and you hadn't brought it up, I definitely would have asked before you dropped me back home."

"Well, we'll talk about it. I'm just hesitant about saying anything because I don't want you to feel like I need you to help me. I want you to know so you'll understand why I was the way I was earlier. This shit is stressing me the fuck out."

"Brixton, why wouldn't you want my help?"

"I suppose I'm saying I didn't want you to think I was asking or hinting around for help by telling you. However, the look on your face earlier, hurt me. Knowing that my distance was the cause of that, I knew I had to tell you more. You're the woman I want a life with. If I can't tell you this, then something is wrong."

She smiled slightly as I pulled my hand away from hers to put the truck in drive to head to Pappadeaux Seafood Kitchen. "I'm listening, Brix."

"Mr. Jeffcoat came to the house earlier today with documents, giving us thirty days to pay forty thousand dollars. After looking at the paperwork, I saw that my parents had borrowed fifty grand years ago and put the house up as collateral. No one told me. I found out about it this morning. I've been spending money trying to put a house and property back together that may no longer be ours next month. I filled out an application online with my bank to see if I can borrow the money."

She was staring at me intently as I told her the real, feeling like I was about to break into a sweat. I turned up the A/C a bit then continued. "My gym hasn't been doing the greatest for the past two years since competition moved into the area. So my debt to income ratio isn't looking the greatest right now. I'm afraid the loan will probably be denied. I'll either have to sell my gym, turn it into something else, or offer some new service to attract clients in order to keep my dignity. I have to do something now, or I'm gonna be sinking within the next three months."

"That's a lot to carry alone, Brix."

"Tell me about it. That's why I wasn't in the greatest mood earlier. I didn't feel like being around anyone but you, but I didn't want to take you away from your people. That was why I went back home. I would have talked to you earlier than now. Nothing has changed about the way I feel about you or the way I see you. You didn't do a thing, and I definitely missed you, baby."

"I'm so sorry about all of this. Is there anything I can do or help you do?"

"You can spend time with me. I know you have to spread yourself thin when you're in Nome, but I hope to spend as much time as possible with you. I have to make a trip to Austin to handle business once you leave, and I'm not sure how long I'll be gone."

"I can do that. Maybe I can help you brainstorm ideas for your gym too."

"I'd appreciate any ideas you can come up with."

When I turned in the parking lot, I noticed a spot up close, so I parked up there. When I got out and walked around to help her out, I saw a frown on her face. After opening her door, she smiled slightly. "You good, Jess?"

"I will be. That muthafucka showed up in Nome again. I'm sick of his bullshit."

"Maybe you need to have a final talk with him."

"That's all the fuck he's gonna get too. I'll talk to his ass again, but I'm sick of talking. I mean, I know he's gonna come to town sometimes because Lennox is his brother, but why does that always have to be when I'm in town? This shit is irritating."

I grabbed her hand and led her to the entrance without another word about Decklan. I knew she didn't want him. I was more concerned about Nate and how that shit went. I didn't want to ask, but I knew it would benefit me to just be a straight shooter with Jess.

Once we got a table and sat, I went right in. "So how was the game and your time with Nate?"

"It was cool. He had a good game, and I got to meet Noah. They talked about David Guillory. He used to be Noah's stepdad and was Nate's father. Nate never got to know him. So we were both in our feelings after that because we were talking about the sins of our mothers. However, I know that's not the shit you really want to know."

I frowned slightly as she gave me a smirk. She wanted to play games. "So tell me the answer to what it is you think I want to know."

"Not until you ask the question, Brix."

I rolled my eyes. She wanted me to be a savage. Once that side of me was out the box, he was gon' stay out. "Okay. Don't get offended when I speak my mind."

MONICA WALTERS

She rolled her eyes. "I won't, as long as you don't get offended by my answers."

I almost didn't want to know after she said that. She would purposely give me too many details. "A'ight. Savage nigga engaged."

She slowly shook her head. "Whatever, Brix."

"Did you fuck him?"

She hesitated, crossing her legs and shit. I knew she was fucking with me, but I needed her to put me out of my misery. My gaze had to be pinning her to her damn seat. Finally, she said, "No. I did stay the night with him though."

Thank God. Something wouldn't let me stop there though. "Did you want to?"

Her eyebrows lifted slightly like she couldn't believe I had the balls to ask that question. She was gon' find out that I had the balls to do a lot of shit. "Yeah. Have you seen him?" she asked with a frown on her beautiful face.

"So what stopped you?"

"First, like I said earlier, the conversation threw everything off. We were feeling emotional. He held me in his arms all night, and we even kissed a few times, but for some strange reason, my mind couldn't stay off this nigga I know back in Nome, Texas, and how his dick took my fucking breath away."

I nodded as the waiter came to the table to get our drink and appetizer orders. After ordering a Swamp Thing and their cajun alligator, Jess's eyes met mine while I ordered a simple Crown and Coke. I hoped she ordered a couple more of those Swamp Things. That shit was gon' have her readier than the Energizer bunny. I was gon' have her ass going and going and muthafucking going. Those raspberry and melon liqueurs and frozen Hurricane and Margarita were gon' hit her ass so hard she wasn't gon' know what the fuck had happened.

As soon as the waiter walked away, I said, "So this nigga's dick that's in Nome must be special as fuck if you were thinking about it while you were with someone else."

"Mm hmm. It packs a nice one-two punch, but I wouldn't tell him that. I can't have his head getting big as this fucking table."

"Hmm. The head in his pants is already throbbing and swelling. What'chu gon' do about it?"

She licked her red lips as her eyes stayed on mine. When I felt her bare foot on my leg, I slumped in my seat somewhat, thankful for the linen tablecloths that hid what was going on. Her foot found my erection and she began sliding it back and forth. "Mmmm," I moaned deeply. "You don't play fair."

"I'm just showing you what I can do. You asked me what I was gonna do about it, didn't you?"

"I shol in the fuck did. I'm loving your response, too, baby. You gon' make me fire off in my pants though," I said as I grabbed her foot. "I promise, you gon' be digesting this shit as soon as we get in the truck."

"Mm. You really promise? Because I will definitely delay the expansion of your family tree by swallowing that shit."

"You so fucking nasty. It won't be delayed. When it's time for the tree to grow, it will. You just make sure you ready when that time comes."

She gave me a half smile as the waiter set our drinks on the table and took our orders for dinner. The minute he walked away, she asked, "So you want me to have your babies, huh?"

"Mm hmm... all ten of 'em."

She nearly choked, and I couldn't help but laugh. "Shiiiid, you got the wrong person for *that* job. I can guarantee that shit."

We laughed more. "Seriously, though, Jess. I'm glad I stayed on your mind. I just hope what I had to say earlier didn't change the way you feel about me. I know you're stable financially and probably want a man that's stable as well. I'm obviously not quite there yet, although I thought I was, but I plan to figure it out soon, even if that means I have to start over."

"Brix, I know you, and I thought you knew me. I'm not that superficial. I know you ain't tryna stick me for my paper. I'm not worried about your financial status. Any of us could go from stable to struggling at any minute. What matters is how we handle the transition of that. You aren't the type to fold, so I know you will find a way out. I know your grandparents' property means a lot to you, because you wouldn't be here if it didn't."

I nodded repeatedly as my mind raced, still trying to figure out what to do, even during conversation with her. I lowered my head for a moment then took a sip of my drink. Jess stretched her hand across the table, so I grabbed it. "I got'chu, Brix. Although we aren't in a committed relationship, I care about you a lot... always have."

As I stared at her, I could see the sincerity in her eyes. I couldn't help but feel a way, knowing that she still had feelings for Nate. "Are you going to see him again?"

"Huh?"

"Are you going to see Nate again?"

She looked away for a moment. "I don't know."

I nodded again as I pulled my hand from hers. I was doing my best to be patient, but when we slept together, it put my body in overdrive. I wanted her so bad. She'd taken a hold of my heart and my balls and wouldn't let go. "Brix... please understand."

"I do. You were talking to him first. I'm just hoping that you'll feel for me how I feel for you."

"I feel strongly for you. I'm just..."

Before she could continue, the waiter appeared with our food. Once he left, she didn't continue. We ate in silence, stealing glances at one another. However, she didn't have to verbalize what the issue was. I already knew. She was afraid of jumping in too quickly. After the heartbreak she'd just endured and was still having to relive every time he popped up, she was gun shy. She'd trusted him, even after her issue with men because of her father, and he hurt her. Now she was taking that shit out on me.

When the waiter came to check on us, I asked for a box. She grabbed his attention before he left and said, "Two please."

I placed my hands palms up on the table, and she put hers in them. "I don't want to think about that right now. I just want to concentrate on how beautiful you are and how grateful I am to be spending time with you. When you go to be with your people, can you come back to me when y'all are done for the night?"

"That's possible. Or you can try to convince me to stay with you."

My eyebrows lifted as she stared at me. I could tell she was feeling emotional and needed me to just love on her. She had no clue just how much I cut for her... just how much I loved her. When the waiter came with our boxes and handed me the check, I reached in my pocket and handed him my card before he could walk away.

The moment he left, Jess said, "I thought I asked to take you out."

"You did, but I wanted to take you out too. Dinner ain't gon' break me, Jess."

She rolled her eyes. "I didn't say it would. I asked you to dinner before I knew about your dilemma, jackass."

I chuckled. "You right. You did, but I got it, baby. What you got for me is better than money though. You know how much it costs to trace your roots? And here you finna swallow all my DNA for a meal at Pappadeaux's. That's a deal I can't pass up."

Her face turned red, and she laughed so loudly she had to immediately cover her mouth with her hands. She swatted my hand and said as she looked around, "You make me sick!"

I laughed until my eyes watered. Our moments like this were plentiful back in high school, and I was glad we could still have them twelve years later. We'd definitely gotten attention from her outburst, but no one seemed to even care. Once the waiter came back with my card and we'd boxed our food, I helped her from her seat and led her back to the truck.

Before I could open the door for her, she grabbed my shirt and pulled me to her. She turned and rested her back against the truck as I pressed against her. Our lips were almost touching, but neither of us made a move to kiss. We just stood there staring at one another. I licked my lips and touched her bottom lip with my tongue. The heels she wore made us the same height, so her lips were right there, begging me to suck the fuck out of them then have them wrapped around something thick and chocolatey.

She slid her hands down my chest until she reached the waistband of my pants. "Unlock the doors, Brix."

I did as she requested but didn't make a move to free her from her position against my truck. Had it been dark outside, I would have had her hike this dress up and finger fucked her right here. I backed away from her, being sure to rub my hard dick against her. My pants were too tight for this shit.

I was happy as hell that I'd gotten my windshield tinted because I was anticipating the action she promised me like a mug. I opened her door and helped her inside then walked around and got inside to find her in my fucking seats without underwear. Her dress was around her waist. "Jess, where the fuck yo' drawz at?"

"The same place I left my morals and good sense... at home."

I bit my bottom lip as I unbuckled my belt, unfastened my pants, and pulled my dick from my boxer briefs. "Bring yo' nasty ass over here."

She did as I said and immediately deep throated my shit, not even taking time to get her mouth wet. That shit was already dripping wet like she'd seen a juicy ass pickle that made her mouth water. I grabbed her ponytail as I reclined my seat some, pulling her off my dick. She spit all the saliva in her mouth on my dick and that nigga looked like he was in a damn bubble bath. "Jess, you a nasty muthafucka. Damn."

I kissed her lips, sliding my tongue in her mouth. The way her saliva was on ten, caused mine to be the same. While I thought spitting in each other's mouths was nasty, I enjoyed this shit. It was different. She wasn't just hocking that shit, it was just flowing from her mouth, as was mine, leaking down our chins. I released her ponytail, and she went back to my dick. I couldn't help but to slap her ass. It was in the air, jiggling as she bobbed on my dick.

I slid two of my fingers inside of her and began stroking her like my fingers could get a nut. Feeling her juices leak down my hand while her saliva was leaking down my dick was the truth. Nobody could tell me that my fingers weren't about to nut right now. "Ahh, fuck! Jess! How the fuck you gon' give me all this shit without giving me your heart, baby? That's okay though. I'll wait for it. It's gon' be mine."

She looked up at me as the tears fell down her cheeks. Right after, the 'gawk' noise came from her lips, and I couldn't stop my kids from running wild down her fucking throat. "Jess, fuuuuck!"

She drained me as dry as a phone that hadn't rang in days. Those dick sucking skills didn't fucking play. She released my dick from her suction as I continued finger fucking her. Her eyes fluttered as she moaned. "That's it, Brix. I'm almost there."

"Naw, baby. You ain't finna cum like this."

I pulled my fingers from her and sucked them clean while scooting my seat back and beckoned her to me by grabbing my dick and stroking it. She straddled me quick as hell and slid down my dick, taking us both out of our misery. "Ooooh shit! Briiiixx! Fuck!"

I brought my hands to her ass and held on for the ride of my life. I relaxed in the seat and watched her take herself to ecstasy. When she started cumming, I sat up and began sucking one of her nipples, only intensifying the trembles coursing throughout her body. "I swear this the best pussy I ever had, baby. Give me all that shit, Jess."

My crotch area was soaking wet. All I was fit to do was go home and take a shower. As Jessica's body started to relax, I began fucking her from below as we'd done in the recliner over a week ago. We needed privacy, and neither of us could get that in Nome. I should have just gotten a room for the night, but neither of us could wait. The walk to the truck was torture, because I wanted to fuck her on top of the table in Pappadeaux.

"Jess, fuck! I'm 'bout to nut."

Before she could respond, I shot off in her depths as my eyes rolled to the back of my head. I couldn't believe we'd fucked right here in the front of the parking lot at Pappadeaux. Had anyone gotten close enough, they would have surely seen us, but at the time, I didn't even give a fuck. I had a one-track mind whenever Jess was around.

She lifted from my dick and pulled her dress down then sat in the passenger seat. My dick was still begging for more. He was always on one in her presence. I stuffed him back in my pants and drove out of the parking lot to Walden Road. "Brix?"

"Yeah?"

"If I got a room, would you spend the night with me?"

"What kind of question is that? Hell yeah. Honestly, I'd drive to Houston and just stay at your place out there."

"Really?" she asked with her eyebrows hiked up.

"Mm hmm."

"That's good to know. Tonight, we can just go to the Eleganté or the Marriott. I don't want to have to wait much longer to get at'chu. I need a bed though, baby. I need to be somewhere unrestricted."

"I feel you, baby. Let's go home and get some clothes and come back," I said.

"Yeah, because there is no way I would feel comfortable going anywhere else feeling all gushy and shit without underwear."

I chuckled then grabbed her hand and kissed it. While sex with her was amazing, I could still only hope that all this went somewhere. She was the one for me, and I could feel it plain as day. I felt like she could too, and that was why she was running so hard in the opposite direction when it came to commitment.

CHAPTER ELEVEN

JESSICA

"Bitch, where the fuck you at?"

"I'm on my way to Beaumont with Brix. I'm sorry, Tyeis, but I needed to be here for him."

"So to hell with our plans? You gon' ditch me for a nigga?"

"Hell yeah. You ain't got a dick, and I don't do pussies."

"Ho!" she yelled, then died laughing. "I'll give you that. Send me Nesha phone number so she can come pick me up. Push come to shove, I'm gon' push up on her ass. She like pussies."

We both hollered with laughter. When we contained ourselves, she continued. "Your uncle is here... the real tall one, going off about some lil boy and his daughter. Your mom is really trying to calm him down, but that nigga ain't hearing it."

"Lawd have mercy. He's there again?" I asked rhetorically. "She needs to call Uncle Jasper for him."

"I think she did. Somebody else just got here. When did you come here? I didn't see your ass blow in and blow back out."

"You were in the shower, and I didn't need you getting out while I was there and hold me up. Brixton was waiting for me with his fine ass."

"Watch yo'self, before you get dicked down in here again," Brix said.

Tyeis was quiet for a moment, then she asked, "Was that Brixton? Bitch, I can't deal with y'all nasty asses. I'm about to finally meet this Decaurey, and I'm ready as hell. Is there anything I should know about him?"

"He's a fool. He's younger than you. No kids. He a light bright nigga... just how you like them."

"First of all, I don't discriminate. I like them all shades of black. But those light brights do have my heart," she added with a chuckle. "Okay. Well, I guess I'll see you tomorrow. Your mama was talking about church. I can tell you now, if I stay out too late or if I get fucked up, she's gonna write me off as one of Satan's helpers. Who goes to church on a Friday anyway?"

"Girl, shut up. Have fun. We just got to our room."

"Okay, nasty."

She ended the call as I chuckled and shook my head. "She sounds fun to be around," Brix said.

"She is. That's why I think her and Decaurey will get along well. I hope they connect."

"I hate that it seems I'm keeping you from them. You sure you don't want to go shower and meet them wherever they're going?"

"I'm beyond sure. I just wanna hear you say I got the best pussy in the world again. Your dick ain't nothing to throw rocks at either. That shit is top tier."

He slowly shook his head as a smirk appeared on his lips. "You ain't gotta stroke my ego. I know my shit on that level. I'll give you whatever you want, Jess. All you have to do is insinuate it. I rock that hard for you, baby, and I truly believe that you know that."

I swallowed back the tears he was trying to pull out of me. Just the fact that I couldn't spend this type of quality time with Nate had me ready to commit to Brix. We could live in the country and raise a family... something I'd always wanted. However, my brain was telling me to take it slow. Every time Decklan's ass came up, it seemed I retreated within myself, and I hated that. He was probably going out with them tonight. That was another reason why I didn't want to be there without Brix.

If Brix couldn't go, then neither could I. His ass wouldn't approach me again if Brix was with me. I couldn't understand why he couldn't just accept the fact that he fucked up and that I was done with him. Years ago, I vowed to myself that I would never let a man mistreat me, nor would I stay in a one-sided relationship. I did that for four fucking months with Decklan. I was the only one making an effort, and it was because he was too busy making efforts with other women.

Brix had a lot going on in his life right now. I didn't know his business was taking a hit too. What if it was too much for him, and he started taking that shit out on me? I couldn't allow myself to end up in the same situation I was in with Decklan. I would have to do a better job at protecting my heart before it wasn't worth having. I didn't want to become bitter and hate men altogether. I wanted to love, and I knew it wouldn't be long before I fell for Brix if we continued the way we were.

"What are you thinking about, baby? You got quiet on me."

"Just what you said earlier about me knowing how hard you rock for me. I do know that, Brix. Your friendship means the world to me. Now that we have leveled up to more than friends, I want to say that this means the world to me too. If I commit to you, I don't want that to change."

"It would change, Jess. It would get better... more intense. If you were mine, you would get all my love, tenderness, support, and loyalty. I'd be devoted to you. I'm not him and couldn't be him, even on my worst day. I'd never fuck around on you. You the cream of the crop. What I look like pulling weeds? If I would do anything for you now, imagine what level that shit would be on if you were mine?"

"Brix, I'm bossy."

"Always been."

"I'm possessive."

"Me too."

"I'm crazy as fuck."

"Once again, always been, Jess."

I rolled my eyes and focused my gaze on the floorboard of the truck. "Brix, although I don't show it, I'm sensitive."

"I know that too, baby. I pay attention to you. I can tell when you're hurting. I can see it every time Decklan's name comes up. I know that's probably why you don't want to kick it with your people. You think he's gonna be with them."

This man knew me so well. I closed my eyes, trying to filter the negativity out of my mind. I wanted to just enjoy my time with Brix. "I want to enjoy time with you, Brix. That's it."

I crossed my legs and surveyed the leggings I'd changed into as he drove in the parking lot of the hotel. "Okay. I'll be right back."

"Brix, let me pay for this. Just like you got me, I got'chu. I told you that. Let me have you now. Okay?"

He closed his eyes for a moment and bit his bottom lip. I could see that accepting help was hard for him, especially from me. He didn't seem to have a problem accepting Uncle Kenny's help building that fence. "Jess, I got it. Okay?"

I sat back in the seat and allowed him to go take care of the room. He'd driven to the Marriott. I knew this shit was going to cost a grip on a Saturday night. His pride was gonna have his ass broke. I wondered what decision my family came up with regarding him. While he was inside, I texted Jakari. *How did everything go?*

I was just about to text you. Uncle WJ has already paid Mr. Jeffcoat. In the morning we're paying off the back taxes. We are going to present Brix with the news tomorrow evening.

I stared at the text message for the longest. I closed my eyes, thankful for the generosity of my family. Uncle WJ always said that God didn't bless us to not be a blessing to someone else. The Hendersons sustained Nome. We were the heartbeat of Nome. As I thought about it, I wished I would have filed paperwork to change my last name to Henderson as soon as I got away from Joseph.

I thought my last name would have been Guilman. For the entire relationship with Decklan, I'd imagined having his chocolate babies that would have black silky hair like him. I had so many hopes and dreams that I'd kept to my fucking self. Maybe if I had been more open with him, he wouldn't have strayed. Maybe he didn't know how serious I was about him and didn't bother to ask. He wasn't as forthcoming about his feelings either. Maybe we did need to have a final conversation.

As I rationalized it in my mind, Brix came back to the car. "They don't have any rooms available. There's some kind of little league select baseball tournament going on."

"Okay."

He journeyed to Elegante, only to suffer the same fate. Everyone was booked unless we chose to sleep in a motel, and I'd be damned. We would just have to go back to his mom's house and be quiet or not fuck at all. There was no way we could go to my parents' house. CJ wouldn't let shit go unknown. The lil boy was always in somebody's business. Most times, my grandmother had him since my parents still worked, but his lil ass was hell on wheels.

Plus, because of how she raised me, I would feel like I was disrespecting her house. She always stressed that I preserved myself for marriage. She was honest about not being a virgin when she got married but that she wished she would have waited. That all went out the window. Honestly, I didn't listen to her words as much as I paid attention to her actions. She always spoke to me in love, and her words helped me later in life whenever I recalled them, but at the time, I wasn't hearing her... just watching.

"Well, I guess we can either go back to Nome, or I can take you to meet your family wherever they are."

"I'll go back to Nome."

Somehow, the mood between us had fizzled, and we both seemed to be in our heads. Neither of us were talking much, and it was moments like this that made me doubtful about getting into another relationship. He headed up Walden Road to get to Major Drive. I wanted to see where he would take me. If he took me to my parents' house, then I'd feel justified with my doubts. I wanted to be in his arms, and I wanted to be with him period, but I just didn't know how this would end up.

"SO YOU CHILLING in the house tonight? It's close to the weekend. I was sure you would be out having a good time."

"Yeah, me too."

Brix had taken me home, and I was feeling depressed. I didn't bother telling him that I wanted to be with him. He'd taken me to the place he wanted me to be. I felt like if he wanted me with him, he would have taken me to his mom's house. Maybe he wasn't comfortable with me being there because of the situation with his mom. I didn't know, but my mind kept trying to come up with excuses for his behavior.

After I got home and had taken a shower, I called Nate. I wanted to go home. Tyeis had messaged me a couple of times, talking about how fine 'thick ass' Decaurey was, and I sent eyeroll emojis every time. She said he didn't seem interested, but she would still subtly let him know that she definitely was. Whatever floated her boat.

"You okay? You sound bothered."

"I am, a lil bit, but it's nothing I can't handle. How was your day?"

"You sure? You know I'm a good listener. My day was cool."

"I know. When will you be back in Houston?"

"Tuesday. But only for one night. Then I'll be back in Dallas."

"I was supposed to head home Wednesday evening, but I may leave Tuesday so I can see you."

"For real?"

"Yeah. Although we were both in our feelings last time, I enjoyed spending time with you, Nate."

"I enjoyed it too, especially holding you all night. That shit felt right to me."

"Yeah. So how long will you be in Dallas?"

"A few days. I have a game next Friday. You coming to Dallas?"

"I don't know. I have a shoot that Friday, but it's only in Houston. After that, I have a two-week break. I thought I would spend it in Nome, but I don't know. I feel like hitting a rodeo or something. I might go to my aunt's house and ride tomorrow. I love the peace it gives me."

"I wish I could come ride with you."

I smiled slightly. That would be hard to accomplish. Aunt Tiff, Uncle Kenny, Uncle Jasper, and Brixton lived on the same highway, walking distance from each other. If Brix saw us, I didn't know how I would handle that... or how he would handle that for that matter. Right now, I just wanted to be loved on, and it seemed I wouldn't be getting that unless I initiated it.

"Me too, Nate. I just wanted to see how you were. I'll call you soon."

"A'ight, baby girl. Can't wait to talk to you again."

I ended the call without responding. Instead of succumbing to depression and misery, I got dressed and headed somewhere that would definitely be entertaining. When I left my room, CJ was running down the hallway in his drawers. I rolled my eyes and went the opposite direction. I was trying to move quickly, but his lil ass saw me anyway. "Jess! Where you going?"

"Mind my business. Why are you still up?"

"Mama let me stay up!"

"No, I didn't, CJ! Get your butt in that bed!" my mama said as she came out of her room.

I slowly shook my head as CJ ran inside his room and closed the door. My mama turned her attention to me and asked, "Where are you headed?"

"To Uncle Storm's house. I just need the drama, or I'm gonna end up high at Uncle Jasper's."

She chuckled, and I did too. "What's going on?" she asked.

"Just trying to deal with Brixton's mood swings. I know he's stressed, so that's why he's getting a pass, but it's causing my mood to fluctuate too."

"Yeah. I understand why now, since you wouldn't tell me."

I smiled slightly. "What made y'all agree to pay the back taxes too?"

"Philly dug into his background. He's a go-getter. We could see that if he just got a fresh start with this, he would do what he had to do to keep it up."

"Wow. That's so amazing. I can't wait until y'all tell him so he can release all the stress he's harboring. That's an amazing blessing for him and his mother."

"It really is, and it felt amazing to approve it. No one was against it, not even Storm."

"That's great. You know, I think I'm going to Uncle Jasper's house, because I might hurt one of those kids with the way I'm feeling."

My mama laughed, then said, "You may wanna call him first. I would hate for you to go over there for him not to answer the door."

She rolled her eyes playfully as I frowned. When realization set in, I laughed. Uncle Jasper and Aunt Chasity were known to get it in whenever and wherever. I couldn't be rolling up on that. "You shol right."

I sent him a text right then. *Hey, Unc. You busy?*

Naw. Sitting on the deck with Shylou and Kenny.

Okay. I'm on my way.

I'd forgotten that fast that Shylou was in town since I told him of Noah's plans for me by text. It wasn't like he hung around me. He was usually with Uncle Kenny. That was his best friend. "He's on the deck with Shylou and Uncle Kenny. So I'm good to roll up on them. I'll see you when I get back, Ma."

"Okay, baby."

I kissed her cheek and headed down the road. As I passed Brix's house, I saw him sitting outside. I didn't stop. He wanted to be alone with his feelings, so that was where I would leave him. It was like because we couldn't find a room, that depressed him and caused him to sink back into his hole about the bullshit that had gone down. I was trying to understand, but that shit was hard for me. Most times, when I was going through something, no one was able to tell... except my mama and Nesha. No one else had a clue, because I went on with my day, pretending nothing was wrong.

When I turned in the driveway, I noticed Uncle Storm's truck. *Lawd have mercy.* Shit was about to be on ten. I already knew it. He was gon' be with the shits. Uncle WJ was here too. I supposed they were having a bruhs' turnup or some shit. That was okay, because I was about to crash that shit. I needed a blunt in the worst way.

I got out of my car and walked around to the back gate. Once I walked in, I noticed Aston, Malachi, Philly, and Uncle Ryder were here, too, and upon further inspection, so were Uncle LaKeith and my dad. I thought he was in the bedroom with my mama. How didn't she know he was here? Well, she probably knew now since Uncle Jasper had only originally said that Shylou and Uncle Kenny were here.

"Hey, baby girl. What'chu doing here?"

"Hey, Daddy. I'm sorry to interrupt y'all's bromance, but I needed to chill out for a minute."

Carter smiled big, and that never got old. It always made me feel good inside to watch him do so. As I walked up the stairs of the deck, Uncle Jasper held out a blunt for me. He already knew what the deal was. Just as I put it to my lips and Uncle Jasper lit it for me, Uncle Storm's ass was hopping on my nerves.

"What the fuck you called this? A bromance? What the fuck is that supposed to mean?"

Aston chuckled. He was a mechanic at Uncle Storm's shop, and his stepdaughter was married to Uncle Marcus, who'd just walked up behind me, slapping people's hands. "Storm, it's just a saying for when men have a brotherhood like we do."

"This shit ain't a brotherhood. It's family. If one of y'all fuck up, I ain't going down for none of y'all. So it surely ain't a brotherhood. I got an election to think about."

I rolled my eyes, and I noticed everybody else did the same. "Nigga, ain't that the same thing?" Uncle WJ asked.

"Naw, 'cause you don't necessarily like everybody in your family. At times, I don't like none of y'all, especially Jasper's ass."

Uncle Storm finally chuckled. He always had to be difficult. I took a pull from the blunt and sat in the empty seat next to Uncle Storm. I closed my eyes then realized how quiet it had gotten. I opened them to see everybody was staring at me. After exhaling the smoke, I said, "Damn. What? I'm not gon' stay the whole time. I just wanted to smoke."

"Shit, you pulled on that shit like you was trying to inhale all of it at once though. You good?" Uncle Marcus asked.

"She probably been around Brix and just as stressed as he is," Uncle Storm said.

I didn't know how he always knew people's business, but his ass did. If he didn't know, he was good at bluffing until he found out. I cut my eyes at him as he put his arm around me. "It'll get better after tomorrow evening. He gon' be set."

I took another pull as my cousin Mal said, "Shit, give me one. The way Jessica smoking that shit and rolling her eyes, it *got* to be fire."

I almost choked from laughing at his ass. When I caught my breath, Uncle Storm said, "You ain't gotta leave. You know we got'chu, Ace. Shiiid, you and Tiff more like one of us anyway. You sure you good?"

"Yeah. He's just having mood swings, and I know it's because he's stressed. It's just making me feel the same way when I'm around him. I hate feeling like that."

"I get it. I saw yo' ex-nigga was in town. You good with that?"

"I hate that his ass is here. It's like he's using the fact that Lennox is his brother as an excuse. It feels like he's lowkey stalking me. This is the second time he's shown up while I was here. I plan to have a last heart to heart with him. After that, I'm gon' go upside his fucking head if he keep popping up on me. Maybe we can do that one day this weekend."

"Sounds like a plan. Let me know when, and I'll be in the vicinity to make sure he don't try nothing."

"Well, I'll probably be at Aunt Tiff's riding. So he'll have to come out and ride with me. I feel like that will help me express myself better. It's so peaceful, and I've been neglecting that side of my personality lately. I miss the country."

"Uh huh. Move yo' ass back. I know you've made enough bread to get you a house. Hell, you can get one in the Henderson Ranch edition with Nesha, Jakari, and KJ. I think Christian, Rylan, and yo' brother looking at building houses out there too. Even Decaurey been looking at moving."

"Yeah, it's a thought. I can work from anywhere, but Houston is more convenient. However, I won't be able to do this my entire life, nor do I want to."

He nodded repeatedly as I killed my blunt. I felt relaxed as hell too. When I stood from my seat, Uncle WJ asked, "You good, niece?"

"Yeah, Unc. I'm good now. Thanks... And thank you for what you did earlier."

He gave me a one-cheeked smile and said, "We gon' always do what we can do for our people. Always."

I walked around and kissed everybody bye then walked to the gate to head to my car and saw Brix leaned against it.

CHAPTER TWELVE

BRIXTON

When she came through the gate and I saw how low her eyes were, I wished I would have gone back there and put one in the air too. The smell was strong, and when the wind blew just right, I could smell the shit at my house. I got that contact high at least once a week. As she got close, she asked, "What are you doing here?"

"I owe you an apology. I don't have a problem expressing my feelings and desires when it concerns you. However, when things aren't going so well, especially financially, in my life, I have an issue with telling anyone, not just you. I don't want you to view me as a failure. I view myself that way, so I can't fault you if you viewed me that way too. It's embarrassing to say the least."

I looked away for a moment as I took a couple of steps backward. She was watching me intently, waiting for me to continue. "While I was trying to get a room at the Marriott, my manager from the gym called, and I officially closed the doors. I sent emails out when I got home. I haven't decided whether I will sell, revamp things by offering shit others aren't offering, or turn it into something totally different. I'm stressed to the max, because that leaves no money coming in."

"Brix..."

WHERE IS THE LOVE

Ignoring her plea, I kept going. "I called movers to get on their schedule. I'll be selling my house in Austin and moving here permanently. It's just a lot, Jess. I'm not telling you this to ask for help. I just wanted you to know why I just seem all over the place. My mental is taking a hit, baby. I'm sorry."

She stepped closer to me then slid her arms around my neck. "You're not a failure. Things will come together. This is just a storm... a test. Keep your faith. Okay?"

I frowned at her slightly. What faith was there to have in this situation? I didn't have the money, and I wasn't looking for a handout. Instead of stating all that because I was in my pitiful feelings, I just said, "Okay."

I kissed her forehead and as I was pulling away, she grabbed my shirt then suddenly released it. "What's up?" I asked her.

"Nothing. I'm sorry."

I stepped closer to her again and tipped her head up by her chin and laid my lips on hers. My hands went to both sides of her face and held her to me like she was gonna get away. Truth was, it felt like she was. I didn't want to lose her because I couldn't control my emotions. She left her last man because of the distance. "Jess, why are you apologizing?"

"Because I was gonna say something, but I thought better of it."

"Can you stay with me tonight, baby? I know it's my mom's place. Soon enough I'll have my own, but I need to hold you. I need you close."

She closed her eyes and took a deep breath. "Are you sure? I don't want you to ask me to come over because it's what you think I want."

"I asked because it's what I want. Is it what you want though?"

She licked her lips then opened her eyes. "Yeah."

I opened her door for her, and she got inside. I walked around and got in the car with her since I'd walked down here, and she drove to my mother's house... her house for the next thirty days anyway. We got out and made our way inside. After locking the door, I grabbed her hand and led her to my bedroom. As soon as I closed the door, she came out of her clothes, leaving her undergarments on. I didn't even think she was trying to be sexy, but shit if she didn't have me about to blast off just from staring at her body.

"Jess, you so fucking fine. Always have been. I don't think I can ever say that shit enough."

"What makes you think so, Brix? I have rolls everywhere and stretch marks on my sides. I'm a big girl, and maybe that's why I can't find love. 'Cause where is it?"

I frowned slightly. Jess was always confident, so this threw me for a loop. That was when I remembered she was high. Maybe these were her constant thoughts. She was good at hiding shit. "Baby, just because you were with a couple of niggas that didn't recognize your worth doesn't mean love is hiding from you. Love is right here in front of you. Your curves are so fucking attractive. Rolls and stretch marks ain't nothing but character."

I walked over to her and went to my knees. After kissing her stomach, I backed her to the bed so she could sit, then I traced every stretch mark she spoke of with my tongue. When I glanced up at her, I could see the tears on her cheeks. *Damn.* "Are you saying you love me, Brix?"

"Yeah. Don't you love me?"

"Yeah... but—"

I put my fingers on her lips. "No buts. Whether you're in love with me or not will reveal itself when it's time. I can feel that you genuinely love me for who I am, and I'm sorry for pushing you away, no matter how short a time that was."

She nodded and scooted in the bed. I took off my clothes and joined her, pulling her close to me. She laid her head on my shoulder and lightly stroked my chest back and forth with her hand. "Why is love so difficult? I mean... if you love someone, shouldn't you want to do right by them?"

"Yeah. If they didn't do right by you, maybe it's because they didn't love you."

"Brix, I feel like it's my fault. I'm not the most expressive person in the world. I'm like a whole ass nigga. I like to fuck and don't offer my true feelings. I loved Decklan and never told him. Maybe if he knew, he wouldn't have cheated on me. If he knew that I imagined myself marrying him, he would have tried harder to be faithful."

"Naw. That ain't on you. If you didn't express your feelings to him, it's because he never made you feel safe enough to do so. If he was your man, he should have made it easy for you to say how you felt. I want to be that man for you one day. I just hope that you eventually see that I *am* that man."

She lifted her head and kissed my lips then sat up and took off her bra. "I can't sleep with this shit on."

And I can't sleep with those hard ass nipples on display. I was tripping from her being in her bra and panties. Now she was making it that much harder. I knew I would be sliding inside of her in just a minute. She licked her lips as she stared at me. My eyes dipped to her nipples, and she decided to tease me further by pinching them and moaning. "Jess, you want me inside of you?"

"No. Your mom is here."

"She's asleep, and we're in my bedroom. You got me sitting here fiending for a taste now."

I grabbed my dick through my boxer briefs and squeezed the head. Jess stood from the bed, and she swayed slightly, like she was dizzy. She was fucked up. Her ponytail swung to her shoulder as she turned around, putting her back to me. When she pulled her underwear off, bending over as she pulled them to her ankles, my dick throbbed more, to the point of being painful. Her pussy was wet as fuck and had spread open for me to drool over.

As she took them off, I went to her side of the bed and sat on the floor behind her. "Jess, come sit that shit on my face."

She turned to me with her panties in her hand. She glanced down at my dick, so I exposed him for her to see. "You have a big dick, Brix."

"Mm hmm. And every inch of him wants to be buried inside of you. You cool with that?"

"Yes, but only after you eat this meal. Don't leave any leftovers, Brix."

I pulled her to me as she widened her stance and slumped some as I stared into her eyes. She didn't hesitate one bit as she lifted her fupa and sat her pussy right on my lips. I did my best to clean the plate without wasting a drop. My slurping noises had gotten out of hand because there was so much to digest. I didn't understand how one woman could flood the area like this. She began sliding her pussy back and forth across my lips and her juices were everywhere but where they should have been... my mouth.

I gripped her ass and held her steady so I could fill up on the greatness she excreted. Damn, she tasted so fucking good. They needed to bottle this shit and sell it in the organic section with the cauliflower pizza and shit. This was the expensive shit that wasn't watered down with chemicals and preservatives. It was all natural and was taking me on a high like that ganja she smoked a little while ago.

"Briiiix, I'm about to cuuuuumm!" she whispered harshly.

I was glad she remembered not to scream. While her screams were sexy as fuck, I didn't need my mama waking up and getting all in our business. I smacked her ass, indicating that I was ready to taste all that shit she had to offer. Right after, the wetness that ensued nearly took me out the game. I could barely breathe because that shit had covered me. I couldn't swallow fast enough, and it was threatening to go up my nose.

I had to pull away and allow her to leak down my chin. Her flavor was dripping from my beard. I yanked her ass down right on my dick. There was no give on this floor so she felt every bit of me. Her nails sank into my arms as I stared at her. My natural bags under my eyes seemed heavier, like they were weighed with passion and anticipation of what she would do to me.

Her mouth formed an 'O' and she began slightly bouncing on it. "Oh fuck," I said quietly.

Jessica's head dropped back, and I swore she fucked the life out of my shit. Her bounce jerked my dick around like he was a lightweight and was teaching him to fuck with somebody safe next time. But shit, I didn't wanna play it safe. Risk had to be my middle name, and I stayed getting singed by the fire it brought. Jessica was lethal. She was killing my shit in every stroke, and she didn't give a fuck. She was concentrating hard too, because she never made a sound.

I had to move her though, because I was about to nut already. I helped her up, then stood and pushed her to the bed. She lay on her stomach and tooted her ass up, so I got behind her and prepared to fall in love with everything her pussy had to give me. Her ass jiggled as soon as I entered her, and my dick twitched in excitement while inside of her. I thought I was in the position of power and would show her some shit, but when she started twerking on me, I quickly realized that my assumption was wrong as fuck.

Watching her pussy grip me and leave evidence of its work all over my dick proved to me that I hadn't had sex until meeting her. This was what this shit was supposed to feel and look like. My dick was supposed to look a different color because of all the creamy shit leaking out of her. It was supposed to be shiny and wet as fuck like I'd dipped him in donut glaze. That also let me know just how much she loved sex with me. I turned her on so much she couldn't contain herself.

"Briiix, oh my God!"

She had gotten loud. I shoved her head to the bed to muffle her moans and wore her pussy out, taking control of the situation, letting her know that just because I was allowing her to run shit didn't mean I was incapable. "Ahh fuck! Jess, I'm about to nut."

Within three strokes, I fired off, and I couldn't even keep my damn balance. I fell on top of her as my dick spasmed within her walls. "Damn, Jess, I love you. I fucking love you so much, baby."

WHEN THE DOORBELL RANG, I left the kitchen as I watched my mama take her roaster pan out of the oven. While we were cordial, I was still somewhat pissed about the position they'd put me in. I'd talked to my sister earlier today, right after Jess left, telling her what was going on. She was in shock and really didn't have much to say. I knew exactly how she felt. The two of us had learned how to budget our money, and I wanted to say that it was because neither of us wanted to be broke like them.

After our phone call, I'd piddled around the house, thinking about how much I enjoyed Jess being here. I was more than sure my mama had heard us at some point, but she hadn't said a word about it. Jess and I had gone two more rounds before we passed out, soaked in her juices. We woke up sticky and still horny. We got it in once more, took a shower together, and got dressed. She left shortly after, although I'd asked her to stay for breakfast. She said her mother had texted to ask her to keep her little brother since her grandmother wasn't feeling well.

So all day, my mind had been on how I told her I loved her. She never responded to me or asked any questions about it. I was so in love with that woman I didn't know if I was coming or going. She had me by the balls without giving me any assurances that we would be together. I had to be a fool.

When I got to the door and checked the peephole, I was surprised to see Jessica's uncle W.J. Henderson standing there. Once I opened it, he smiled. That was when I noticed all the Henderson siblings and a couple more were standing outside with him. There were like twelve of them. That shit made me nervous for some reason, because I didn't have a clue of why they were here.

"Hey, Mr. Lewis. I think you know who I am, but I'll introduce myself anyway. I'm Wesley Henderson, Junior, and these are my siblings, Jenahra, Chrissy, Kenny, Storm, Jasper, Tiffany, and Marcus. I think you also know my nephew, Jakari. That's my sister-in-law, Chasity. She also runs our business office. That's Philly. He works in the business with Jakari on marketing, financials, and whatnot. I'm sure you know my daughter, Nesha."

I nodded at her and Jakari. "Well, I'm Brixton, but everyone calls me Brix. Mr. Lewis died last year." Only my employees called me Mr. Lewis. As of right now, I didn't have any employees anymore. "Would y'all like to come in?"

"Please?"

I stepped aside and invited all of them inside as my mama stared, her eyes stretched open as widely as they could be. That let me know that she didn't have a clue as to why they were here either. I wanted to shoot Jessica a message to see what was going on, but I'd left my phone on my dresser. Once I closed the door and turned to them, I said, "This is my mother, Helen Lewis."

Everyone spoke to her, and she spoke back then turned to tend to her food before she burned the house down. After she turned the fire off, she turned back to us as I walked over and stood next to her, waiting to see what this was about. W.J. looked around at his siblings, and everyone smiled, even mean ass Storm.

"Yesterday morning, I had words with Mr. Jeffcoat. He was telling me that he was about to own these twenty acres if a debt wasn't paid. That didn't sit right with me. So I had Philly look into some things, and I saw that there are back taxes on the property as well. I called a meeting with the family that's present, yesterday evening."

I frowned. I was upset that Mr. Jeffcoat was running his mouth about our private affairs, but there was nothing I could do about it. The affluent bragged and shared their business dealings amongst each other all the time. I wasn't sure if that was how the Hendersons rolled, but I knew the white folks around here did that shit, especially if they were acquiring something from someone that was black.

"In the meeting, we talked about what we could do to help the situation. I hate to see our people struggling. Believe it or not, I've been there. Not knowing where the next meal would come from was hard as hell, especially when you have kids to tend to. I'm not faulting you, Mrs. Lewis, for doing what you had to do to survive. Since we are in a position to help, I knew I didn't want to see him take your land from you. Plus, I know you're interested in my niece."

Oh shit. Did Jess say something to him about my dilemma? I could feel my anger rising inside as I listened to him talk about how they dug into my financials and saw I was having a hard time with the gym and that I had no revenue. I was about to boil over and strike out. My financials were my fucking business. I told Jess that shit in confidence. I stopped dead in my pursuit of words to say when he said, "We took care of everything."

"What?" I asked, confused as hell.

"The family agreed that we should take care of it. We paid Mr. Jeffcoat yesterday evening and took care of the back taxes this morning. Your property is free and clear. It's up to you to keep the taxes up. We see you're a businessman, so we know you'll find a way to generate revenue. If you need help getting off the ground with whatever you decide to do, we're here to help."

My mama burst into tears, and Mrs. Jenahra went to her and hugged her as she winked at me. That wink really put me on edge. I turned back to W.J., and said, "Mr. Henderson, I appreciate your generosity, but I don't understand. Will you have a stake in our property? If something were to happen to my mama, will the Hendersons own this property? I'm just confused as to why you would put out so much money for someone if you have nothing to gain from the situation."

"Shiiid, I wondered the same thing," Storm said as Jasper nudged him.

W.J. frowned as he stared at me. "Do you believe in blessings? Reaping what you sew? Any of that shit? We did this to help you. We will get our blessings on the other end. The black community of Nome is struggling. People are moving out to more affordable places. That's why Nesha wanted to build the community. We are about helping our people succeed, because the white man surely ain't gon' do it."

I nodded. "Thank you. I really don't know what else to say."

Truth was, I was still struggling with accepting the help. I felt like Jessica had probably had a hand in this, and I didn't like that. I told her that I wasn't asking for help.

"I can see your wheels turning," Jakari said as he shook my hand. "There's no catch, man." He handed me all the receipts for everything they paid. "Besides, you prolly gon' be family anyway. Jess is really feeling you. You gon' go out tonight with us?"

"I don't know. We'll see."

I wasn't going anywhere. I had to talk to her. This didn't feel good, and I didn't know if she had something to do with it or if I was overthinking. Then something she said came to mind. *"You're not a failure. Things will come together. This is just a storm... a test. Keep your faith. Okay?"*

She knew.

CHAPTER THIRTEEN

JESSICA

I was so ready to go out and turn up. My mental was clear, and my body was beyond satisfied. Brix had put it to my ass last night. I wanted to scream so bad. He'd pushed my face in the pillow several times. I hated to leave this morning, but Mama needed me to watch CJ. Grandma said she just felt sluggish and weak. Grandpa had been tending to her all day. When I called to check on her, he was feeding her some soup.

CJ had run my nerves raw. He wasn't knowledgeable on my 'beat a kid ass' policy. I whupped his lil ass when I caught him playing in my shit. He had my clothes all over the place, and that was a no-no. I didn't play about my money, my family, my man when I had one, and my fucking wardrobe. He was risking his life. Then he wanted to cry and scream that he was gon' tell Mama, like I wasn't a whole ass adult.

Tyeis thought the shit was funny. She was still sitting here laughing about it. "If you ever have kids, I feel sorry for their lil asses already. If they are anything like you, they gon' stay getting their asses whupped."

"Shut up, Ty. You ready to show Decaurey what he's missing?"

"Hell yeah. You seen what dress I'm wearing? That shit fit my body like a glove, and it has holes on the sides up to my honey dew melons. If this shit don't catch his attention, then I know something."

"Something like what?"

"His ass is swinging for the other team, because ain't no way he'll be able to overlook all this body I'm gon' be serving."

I laughed as I heard my phone ringing. I was sure it was Brix. I hadn't talked to him in a few hours. I knew the family had left their house already, because Jakari had messaged in our group thread asking about where we were going tonight. I picked up the phone from the dresser and answered. "Hello?"

"Can you meet me at the house for a minute?"

"I was about to get dressed. Are you coming with us tonight?"

"Jess, I need to talk to you. Now."

He ended the call, and I frowned hard as I stared at the phone. What the fuck was he on? I was just in a good mood, thinking about last night and how much fun we would have with everybody tonight. "You good, sis?" Tyeis asked.

"Brix just demanded that I go to their house and hung up in my face."

"Oh shit."

"Oh shit is right. He's clearly got me fucked up. I'll be right back, because I need to let him know he done fucked with the wrong one."

I stormed out of the house. Brix had to be tripping. He had me fuming. I got in my car and burned off, not bothering to tell anyone other than Ty where I was going. She would fill them in. When I got there, he was outside, pacing back and forth. Nothing in Nome was more than a few minutes away, so I got here quickly. He lived on the same highway as my mama, but he lived on the other side of it where the name changed from 326 to 365.

I got out of the car and slammed the door then stormed up to him. "This is the first and only time you gon' demand shit out of me and hang up in my face. You haven't met this Jessica, but this is gonna be your fucking introduction. Don't let the fact that you've known me—"

"Did you tell them?" he asked, cutting off my rant.

"What?"

"Did you tell them?" he enunciated.

"Tell who what?"

"Your family. Did you tell them about my dilemma?"

"No. I wouldn't do that. You wouldn't even let me pay for dinner."

"Did you know?"

I looked away. Jakari had told me earlier that day when he'd met me at the diner then left when he saw my people were with me. When I didn't answer, he nodded repeatedly. "So that shit about having faith and that it would work out was you basically telling me what was going on."

"Brix, Jakari told me about it at the diner after you left. Yes, I knew. I also knew about the meeting and that they would most likely handle it. What's wrong with accepting help?"

"Nothing is wrong with help unless somebody betrays your loyalty to get it for you. You didn't ask for it, but you definitely encouraged it. I'm a man, Jess. I don't need your influence to take care of my shit. Your uncle even mentioned that one of the reasons they were helping me was because of my interest in you!"

I was so angry my nose was twitching like a growling dog. "You know what? Don't accept it then. You and your mother can move out and live on the fucking street then, Brix. Fuck outta here with that shit. If you too proud to accept help, then you aren't the one for me like I thought. Thank you for showing me that shit early on."

"If you can't respect me as a man, then maybe you're right."

"Nigga, fuck you."

That hurt me to my heart to talk to him that way. He was tripping. I had nothing to do with that shit. I walked away, and he allowed me to do so. I got in my car and burned off out of the gravel driveway, probably throwing rocks in my wake. *Where is the love?* I was fucking right. Love avoided me. He just told me he loved me last night. I knew he meant he was in love with me, but this shit today wasn't love.

When I got back to the house, I went straight to the stairs as my mama and Carter stared at me. When I got to the room, I pulled out the sexiest dress I had then grabbed my phone. *Let's go to the hip hop club in Beaumont.*

We rarely went to that shit because the majority of the crowd was younger. My phone started going off back-to-back.

Nesha:(Soldier Boy meme) The hip hop club!

Decaurey: Who done fucked wit'cho ass?

Jakari: I got a feeling. Jess, don't be naked.

Nesha: Damn, like that Jakari? She that mad?

Jakari: If it's about what I think it might be, hell yeah.

Decaurey: See, she gon' have me getting kicked out the club for fighting.

Nesha: LOL! Nigga, you ain't gon' be fighting.

I rolled my eyes and put my phone on the dresser then sat on the bed. I lay down and stared at the ceiling then curled into the fetal position. My core was struggling. I wanted to lay in bed the rest of the day and then hit the road to go home tomorrow. I was so disgusted. Here I was, about to choose Brixton over Nate. Maybe I was just meant to be single for the rest of my life. Love wasn't meant for me.

Ain't no man want a woman that's aggressive. You sit there and shut up. He handles the business of the house. Your job is to make sure it's clean and that he has a meal cooked after he's worked a long day. All that back talk is what got you slapped. I will beat that shit right out of you, so you best get it together, Jessica. I mean it.

Joseph's words to me the first time he slapped me in the face had come back to memory and haunted me. Apparently, he was right. The men in my life weren't shit. I was the problem. I got up and grabbed my phone to send a text to Decklan. I closed my eyes for a moment, then sent it. *Are you still in town?*

Hey, Jess. Yes. I'm leaving Sunday.

Meet me at Aunt Tiff's house tomorrow afternoon around three to ride.

Really? Okay.

I brought the phone with me to the bed as someone knocked on the door. "Come in."

Tyeis walked through the door, and my mama was right behind her. Neither of them said a word. My mama got in bed with me and held me in her arms like she used to do when I was little. Tyeis sat on the chair in the corner and allowed tears to fall from her eyes as she watched me. I assumed her tears were because she could feel my pain. She'd never seen me this way... feeling so broken. It stayed quiet for a while. I hadn't dropped a tear. The old Jessica that had tried to resurface after connecting with Brix was gone. I was back to normal again, but I wasn't really happy about it.

I swallowed hard then said, "I'm okay, Mama."

"Are you sure? Do you want to talk about it?"

"I'm sure, and no, I don't want to talk about it."

I pulled away from her and got out of the bed to go start the shower. We would be leaving in a couple of hours, and I needed to get ready. I didn't want to be rushed, so it was best that I started now. I closed the door to the bathroom and messaged Nate. *Hope you're having a great day. Can't wait to see you Tuesday.*

I was just thinking about you. I'm in Miami about to put this work in. I wish you were here with me. I miss you.

I smiled slightly then responded. *I miss you too. Good luck tonight.*

Thank you, baby.

Nate was so sweet, but I felt bad about talking to him now. It seemed like I was only talking to him because I was pissed at Brix. I really wasn't using him. I was just lonely. I was contemplating being with him when I first reconnected with Brix. That was why I hadn't committed to him. So if anything, I should have been grateful that Nate was in the picture, or I would have made another dumb ass mistake to let another man make a fool of me.

"I KNEW YO' ass was gon' wear something that pushed the line like a cow trying to eat grass on the other side of the fence."

"Shut up, Jakari."

I strutted my thick ass right by him in a strapless sequined dress that hugged my body and was as short as I could stand it. I wouldn't be doing any bending over in this shit, or my whole ass would be out. When I sat, I had to keep my legs down and together. If I crossed them, I would give everybody a show. This wasn't a free for all.

When we got to the entrance, the bouncer took one look at Tyeis and me and said, "Damn. Where the fuck y'all came from?"

"H-Tine, baby," Tyeis said.

Her ass knew she didn't talk like that. "Well, y'all the finest muthafuckas I done seen all night. Y'all come on in here."

"We ain't by ourselves. My cousins are with us," I said as I glanced back at Nesha, Jakari, and Decaurey.

"It's cool, baby. They can come through too. Where you from?"

"Big City Nome, Texas, nigga. What'chu know about it?"

"Not a muthafucking thang, other than y'all mo' country than a sugar sammich 'round them parts. My cousin is from China, and he used to rodeo with a nigga from Nome."

"What's his name?"

"My cousin is Zayson."

"Oh! He's close to my uncles. Red and Legend are too. My aunt rodeos. She has her own relay team."

"Don't tell me your aunt is the hood famous Tiffany Henderson Semien."

"Hell yeah. That's my mama's baby sister. She more like my big sister instead of my aunt."

"That's what's up. You cool as fuck. I'ma come find yo' pretty ass later."

"Mm hmm. Do that," I said as I walked past him and joined my crew inside the door.

Jakari gave me the side eye. "I knew you was gon' be on that bullshit tonight, but I feel you. Let's get to VIP so we can find a seat."

We had a standing presence in VIP, although we hadn't been here in a while. Whenever we came, we just had to show our IDs, and they'd let us past the rope to go upstairs. When we got to the staircase, Jakari and Nesha took out their IDs as my phone vibrated in my bra. I slightly rolled my eyes but changed my whole attitude when I saw it was Nate. I smiled as I opened his message. *Half time. We up by ten. Just wanted to holla. You still my good luck charm although you ain't here. I got fifteen points.*

Congratulations! Good luck on the second half.

I responded quickly and got my ID from my bra as the guy at the staircase stared at me. I did that shit slowly too. I was a whole ass flirt. These muthafuckas couldn't do shit for me. Men were the fucking devil, and I was sick of their asses. Right now, Nate was the only exception. However, I was more than sure with time, he would prove to be a fuck up too.

Brix wasn't being fair to me at all. I didn't say anything to anybody about his dilemma. They knew about it before I did. So he was angry that I knew they were planning to handle shit and didn't tell him beforehand, and that him being interested in me gave them more incentive to do something about it. I knew he didn't believe me when I said I didn't say anything, but at this point, he could kiss my ass.

I refused to dwell on all the beautiful words he'd said to me over the past couple of weeks. I just hated I was so fucking vulnerable with him last night. Me being high had my lips loose as fuck. I should have stayed at Uncle Jasper's house and chilled with my uncles and their friends. He was in the same boat with Decklan as far as I was concerned. They'd both said they loved me but turned their backs on me and hurt me.

The bouncer let me and Tyeis past the rope, and as soon as we found somewhere to sit, she sat right next to Decaurey. He licked his lips and glanced down at her cleavage, taking her bait. I was glad the funk I was in hadn't rubbed off on her. She hadn't been joking with me too much because of what she witnessed earlier. Although I wasn't crying, she said she could tell that my soul was hurt by the way I was laying in bed.

Jakari sat next to me and said, "He's always been proud. I didn't think he would lash out at you, baby. I'm sorry, Jess. I knew you were really feeling him."

"It's okay. I thought I had found love, but he proved that he wasn't shit. Fuck that nigga."

He put his arm around me as Nesha sat in front of me on the ottoman. She grabbed my hand and said, "We need to dance to this shit. Come on."

They were playing 2 Pac. She knew that was my nigga. Most rappers I listened to were southern. He was the exception. They were playing one of my favorites too. "How Do U Want It" went hard any day. I stood from my seat as Jakari sat back and watched us dance. Nesha was dancing up on me like she was a nigga, getting me all amped up.

Before long, I was laughing and cutting up. As I almost got carried away, I saw Tyeis and Decaurey dancing together. She looked so happy, and I was happy for her. I just hoped she would be ready to leave early. I refused to stay in Nome until Wednesday morning and constantly be reminded of how Brix broke my heart.

Just like he said he would, that fine ass bouncer found my ass. He stood at the landing and watched me shake my ass in front of Nesha while she slapped it repeatedly. We were having fun, and I wished my cousins could stay with me and keep my feelings out of the dumps. "He is watching you hard. You know what they say... You can get over one nigga by getting up under another one."

I glanced at Nesha to see the smirk on her face. She was trying to cheer me up, because that wasn't something she would say. She was always trying to be encouraging and positive. She didn't encourage ratchet ass behavior. I glanced at her again and said, "What the fuck. Might as well."

CHAPTER FOURTEEN

BRIXTON

I was outside putting out feed for the cattle, when a truck pulled into the driveway. I was in a fucked-up mood and just ready to get out of Nome for a little bit. I wasn't fond of people being all in my fucking business, so that was one thing I didn't miss about being home. Until now, I had no business to really tell, so I was able to fly under the radar. However, it was just like the Lewis's to be the laughingstock of Nome amongst the white folks.

I was embarrassed, and I didn't know how to accept help because I never really had any. I had to work for everything I had. Besides my Pell grant, I had to take out a couple of loans to finish school. My parents didn't have some lavish savings account for Stacy and me. We literally had to pull ourselves up by the damn bootstraps. That shit wasn't easy, but we made it.

It took a lot of discipline and determination to be better than our family had been. She and I agreed that we would succeed by any means necessary. I stood up straight and saw Kenny walking up to me. I wanted to roll my eyes, but the Hendersons had been nothing but helpful. When he got close, I said, "Hey, Kenny. How are you?"

"I'm good. A little tired, but I wanted to stop by on my way home to see how you were and if you needed any help with anything."

"Yeah, I saw that wreck at the light. So you had plenty of action with the ambulance service."

"Yeah, I did."

"I'm doing okay. I don't need anything. I'm just trying to decide what to do with my gym. I thought I was going to move back, and I still might. My thoughts are all over the place. I was thinking that I could just sell it and use the money to do something else. I could also save the money and just go look for a job. I just haven't worked for anybody in a long time. I may not be a good employee."

He chuckled. "I honestly think it would be easier for you to just move back home since you're trying to take care of things out here. It'll be much easier on you. That way you won't have to be worried about what's going on in Austin while you're here and vice versa. You could always use that money to start a different business out here."

"Yeah, I just have to figure out what type of business that would be. I have to go to Austin next week to put things in motion."

We stood there awkwardly quiet for a few seconds, then he asked, "So what's up with you and my niece?"

"Nothing. We just cool."

"Tell that lie to somebody that's gon' believe it. I saw y'all outside at Jasper's house. People that's just cool don't kiss... not like y'all did."

I lowered my head, suddenly feeling guilty about how I spoke to her. "I got mad at her about yesterday, thinking she told y'all about my dilemma. I know what Mr. W.J. said, but I assumed the worst. I could tell by some things she said that she knew y'all were coming to my aid. I was rude to her, and she pretty much told my ass off and left."

"Pride will be your downfall if you let it. A small dose of it ain't bad, but when it causes you to sever meaningful relationships, it's a problem. You can't allow it to control you like that. I can promise you, Jess didn't say a thing to any of us. If she knew about what we were doing beforehand, either her mama or Jakari told her. Do you love her?"

I slid my hand over my face, realizing how I had fucked up. "I do, but I'm more than sure she thought it was all a game now. She just got out of a fucked-up relationship, so what I did to her yesterday was probably reminiscent of what she went through with Decklan."

"Only one way to find out. Call her. Text her. Pop up on her. Whatever you have to do to talk to her and apologize, do it. She's stubborn, but I can tell how much she's feeling you."

I nodded as I listened to what he had to say. Kenny wasn't that much of a talker. When he came to help with the fence, we only talked about shit pertaining to that or the farm. Other than that, he was quiet. So for him to impart his wisdom on me meant that he fucked with me and thought I was an asset to Jess.

"You're right. Thank you."

"You ain't gotta thank me. I'll holla at'chu later. I'm gon' try to brainstorm on ideas for a business venture for you. That may help get your mind flowing with more ideas," he said as he backpedaled.

"I appreciate that."

When he got in his truck, I looked to see it was almost ten in the morning. Even if Jess wasn't awake, maybe she would see my text when she woke up. *Good morning. I'm so sorry. Can we talk?*

No.

She responded immediately. I wasn't expecting that. If she went out last night, I knew they probably got home late. That one-word answer felt like it pierced me right in the heart. I knew she was angry when she left here yesterday. The way I spoke to her didn't exhibit the love I claimed to have for her the previous night. *How could I speak that way to the woman I loved?*

There was no sense in hanging around here today, doing nothing. I could go to Austin today and come back to town Monday evening or Tuesday. That would give me time to talk to my employees in person to tell them how much I appreciated them and how they thugged it out with me until the end. Trying one last text for the day, I sent, *Please, baby. I fucked up. I love you.*

Yes, you fucked up. Have a nice life, Brixton.

That was it for the day. Whoever said that a man couldn't handle the shit he dished out was telling the absolute truth. Her rejection was taking me low. I could only imagine how she felt yesterday when I did it to her. *Damn.* I made my way inside after putting up the feed and took a shower then packed a bag. I'd let this financial bullshit ruin something that wasn't replaceable… my future with her and, just as important, her friendship.

"THANK YOU, Mr. Lewis, for taking the time to come talk to us. Don't let the glares and angry dispositions discourage you. I've been through this before. They didn't even bother telling us. We showed up to work the next day only to see the doors were locked, and they had gone out of business. While you didn't give much of a warning, I knew it was coming. Business has been really slow for the past year. I appreciate you taking the time to come out and talk to us."

Terrence extended his hand and shook mine as I nodded. This shit was hard. Looking at the facility I worked my ass off to build was depressing as hell. It no longer had a heart. The pulse was dead. I walked around the building, wishing I would have been more proactive. The situation with my parents had taken precedence. My dad's death had taken my attention completely. Living in Nome didn't make it any easier. It was hard to see the reality of what was happening since I wasn't here.

I'd called a realtor, and they would be here first thing Monday morning to look at it. There was already a for sale sign on my place, and the movers would be arriving Monday to start packing shit. My bedroom suit would be the last shit to go. They said they would be done Tuesday morning. I would head back to Nome soon after.

At first, I was gonna have my stuff put in a storage unit in Austin, but I knew it would be in my best interest to go ahead and transport it to Beaumont now. That way whenever I figured out what the fuck I would do, it would already be there. As I continued to walk around the place, my phone rang. When I saw Stacy's number, I answered. "Hey, sis. How are you?"

"Hey! Sounds like I should be asking you that question. You good, Brix?"

"I just put my gym up for sale."

"Shit. As if you don't have enough to deal with. I'm sorry. Did you ever hear back from the bank about the loan?"

"Yeah. I didn't get it. My debt-to-income ratio was too high. With the sale of the gym and my house, that should fix that. It doesn't matter though. The Hendersons paid off everything."

"What?"

"The Hendersons paid off everything, including the back taxes in Jefferson and Hardin Counties."

"What the fuck? What do they want in return?"

"Nothing. Mr. W.J. said they didn't like to see the black people of the community struggling. They've been blessed to be a blessing to others. That was nearly a hundred grand they broke off for us to keep that property."

"Damn, bruh! That's a huge weight lifted. Thank God!" After she calmed down, she asked, "Why don't you sound excited about it?"

"I am excited. That's less we have to worry about."

"Naw, Brix. What's up?"

"I told you. I just put my gym and house up for sale. I'm not in the best mood, Stacy."

I didn't want to tell her about Jessica. Everyone close to me knew how much Jess meant to me. Not only did I feel like a failure in life, I felt like a failure in love too. She was right to question where love was. It seemed it was nonexistent by my actions. Depression was descending on me heavy, and that shit was all on me.

"I'm sorry. I'll call you later, okay?"

"A'ight."

"I love you, Brix. Look at this as a new beginning. Things will get better."

"I love you too."

I ended the call and continued walking around. As I looked at my reflection in the mirror as I walked, I couldn't help but think about my father. I looked just like him. In my moment of failure and weakness, I saw him clearly, because in my eyes, he was a failure. It was at this moment I realized my thinking was all fucked up. My father had it hard because his parents had it hard, but he wasn't a failure.

He had a family that loved and supported him. Secondly, he never gave up. When something didn't work out the way he thought it would, he would try something else. He never stopped trying to provide for his family, and that shit made him a grown ass man. It made him honorable and admirable. No matter how high the chips were stacked against him, he tried his best to overcome. When he didn't, he couldn't wallow in defeat like it seemed I was on the verge of doing. He had a wife and two children by the time he was my age.

He had three people depending on him to provide a life for them. We didn't see the tireless efforts he put in or the sacrifices he made at the time. We were selfish kids. All we saw were the things we had to go without instead of being grateful for the shit we had. My parents weren't good at budgeting money, but there were *plenty* of people who weren't. They did the best they could by us. I realized that my attitude toward them and how they handled money was probably why they borrowed it from Mr. Jeffcoat without telling me.

For the first time in a long time, I cried. I sat on the weight bench and let my fears, insecurities, and feelings of inadequacy flow down my cheeks uncontained. I didn't try to dry them up or hold them inside. It was time out for trying to be hard. I needed to be real. I would accept this round one defeat and regroup to start again like Stacy said. Life wasn't over. It was just beginning again.

When I had nothing left inside of me, I grabbed a paper towel from the dispenser and wiped my face. I looked around once more then made my way to the door. After walking out, I noticed all my employees were still standing there. I locked up and turned to them, and the applause erupted. I was glad I had gotten out all my emotions a minute ago, or they would have had me crying right here.

I made my way down the few stairs, and Sherise said, "Thank you, Mr. Lewis, for being a good employer. I wish you the best in your future endeavors."

I nodded and gave her a tight smile and looked at everyone else and did the same. Terrence had probably gotten to them and made them see how much worse this process could have been and how it was so hard for me to let go. They dispersed as I walked to my car. When I got to it, I could see how puffy my eyes were. They looked damn near closed.

I got inside and took a deep breath then messaged Stacy. *You were right. I apologize for my attitude.*

It's okay, Brix. I know you need time to process everything. I'll call later. I have to show a house.

I didn't bother responding to her text. However, after my release, I knew I needed to talk to my mama again. I attacked her without understanding the situation and how I played a part in their decision to keep that loan from me. I closed my eyes momentarily then started my car. I knew my mama would forgive me, so I wasn't worried about how that talk would go. The other woman in my life wouldn't be so easy to convince.

I wished I could take back everything I said to her. If she chose to move on in life, I would have to somehow be okay with it. Whether I wanted to or not, I would have to respect her decision and move on.

CHAPTER FIFTEEN

JESSICA

"You sure you okay, boo?"

"I'm okay, Aunt Tiff. I'm just dreading this conversation I'm about to have with Decklan. It's the last one I plan to have, but I plan to be the most open than I've ever been with him."

"Why? Do you even owe his ass a conversation?"

"I don't owe him shit, but I think it will help him stop low key stalking me, thinking he has a chance. He's disrupting my peace, but I think this conversation will help him understand and help me accept accountability for some things."

"Okay, well, he's driving up now."

She rolled her eyes and walked away. Aunt Tiff was like my big sister. She always had my back, no matter what. I stayed with her whenever I came to Nome when Joseph was still alive. Although I wanted to stay away from home, I couldn't go without seeing my family. My mama needed me to vent to at times, and so did my brother. Plus, I needed to see Nesha and my aunts, uncles, and grandparents.

When Decklan got out of his car, his eyes immediately met mine. Sorrow nearly overtook me. Whenever I saw him, it took something out of me, and I knew that was because I wasn't over what happened. I'd been making that shit look easy too. As much as I hated what he did to me, it was hard to walk away. That was why it took me four months. I didn't want to give up on us, but now that I had, there was no going back.

Once he got close, he gave me a small smile and said, "Hey, Jess."

"Hey," I said, reaching out for his hand.

His eyebrows lifted slightly as he slid his hand in mine, and I led him to the stable where the horses were. Since I was more experienced, I got on Aunt Tiff's horse, Terminator, just in case he got a hair up his ass and decided to buck. Decklan saddled his horse the way I'd taught him to, and we mounted up in silence. As we rode to the pasture, I could see Uncle Storm's truck pull into the driveway. He, Uncle Marcus, and Uncle Jasper got out of it and made their way to Aunt Tiff's back porch.

I smiled slightly as they sat then turned my head to Decklan. He was watching me, probably waiting to see what this was about. I stopped stalling and took a deep breath, exhaling slowly. "Decklan, there are some things I need to say to you that I haven't said. This isn't about us getting back together, because that ship has sailed."

He nodded. I continued since he didn't say anything. "I am so closed off. It takes me a while to verbalize my feelings. I realized that maybe had I verbalized them to you, we would have been in a different space. I saw myself marrying you one day. I had fallen in love with you."

I closed my eyes, and when I felt his hand in mine, I opened them to see him riding close and his glossy eyes on mine. It looked like a tear would drop at any moment. Still, he remained silent. "I believe had I told you how I felt, things would have been different. I'm sorry for being so closed off and unexpressive. It hindered our relationship in so many ways. I never wanted a permanent boyfriend. I saw us making it, even after things started getting weird."

A tear fell down my cheek, breaking through the wall I thought I'd put up. I stared up at the sky, trying to contain myself. When I felt the horse stop, I looked over to see Decklan sliding off his horse. He walked over to mine and got on behind me, then slid his arms around me. The wall fell down from the weight, and I cried uncontrollably for a minute.

Once I calmed down, I said, "So our breakup wasn't totally on you. I contributed to it. I'm trying to be better, but I feel like I just wasn't meant for love. Maybe I was meant to be alone."

"Jess," he said in my ear.

I closed my eyes as he kicked Terminator to get him to walk. His arms felt good wrapped around me. His affection felt like it used to. His forehead rested on my shoulder, and that shit only made me cry more. "Decklan, my father abused me at every turn. He made me feel like my worth was dependent on a man. Like I was only here to serve. He verbally abused me all the time, and he hit me a few times. Because of that trauma, I never wanted to reveal my true feelings for fear of getting hurt or them not being reciprocated. While I thought I was being strong and protecting myself, I realized that it was hindering me and made me weak in a sense."

"What happened between us wasn't your fault. You were perfect, Jess. I was the asshole. I got lonely while you were gone, and I fucked up. After that one time, it was like I severed our connection. We had something so special, and I fucked it up. Then I couldn't stop because things between us weren't the same. The vibe was shot to hell because I'd introduced someone else to parts of me that should have only been yours. That isn't your fault, baby. If I needed more from you, I should have said so."

His arms were still wrapped around me tightly as I sniffled. My phone vibrated, so I pulled it from my bra to see a couple of messages. One was from Nate, and the other was from Brix. Even after expressing myself with Brix, he still hurt me. That was how I knew that love just wasn't in the cards for me right now.

"Jess, you didn't have to tell me you loved me. Whenever you were near, I felt it. It wasn't until a couple of months before we broke up that I could no longer feel it. I believe that was because I had so much hell in me, your light couldn't get through. Don't base your future on the past. I'm sorry about your upbringing. That couldn't have been easy, but you are destined for greater. You'll love again, and the next man will deserve your love."

He kissed my cheek as we continued to ride. Thankfully, Aunt Tiff's horses were well trained. I barely had to do anything for him to keep walking. "Decklan, thank you for that. This transition has been hard. You popping up on me has been hard as well. I think it's because this conversation was needed."

"Yeah, it was. I'm sorry. I just didn't know how to let go, even though I'm the one that fucked up. I'm sorry for the hurt I put you through. I had no idea you were hurting this badly. I'm glad you chose to be vulnerable with me. I won't pop up on you anymore. Besides, Lennox jumped my ass about being here. That nigga told me if I kept following you, he was going to help you file charges."

I chuckled. Since Lennox was a detective, I was sure that Decklan took that threat seriously. This really felt better than I thought it would. It was like a huge weight had lifted from my heart. It felt like we were friends again, and I was okay with that. "I think it bothered me so much because I hadn't been totally open with you. That wasn't fair to you."

"Again, you were perfect. I was the fuck up. I suppose I have more of my father running through me than I thought."

He and Lennox's father was MIA for most of their lives but had finally gotten his act together and had been around for the past couple of years or so. When Decklan and I met, they were just rekindling their relationship with him. "Are you and the guy I saw you with trying to establish something?" Decklan asked, breaking me away from my thoughts.

"I thought we were until he had me fucked up yesterday. I've known him since school, but I feel like we should have taken time to get to know one another more as adults. He's the one that has me in my damn feelings. However, I know I was easily hurt and offended because I hadn't properly handled the situation between the two of us."

"So what are you gonna do?"

"I think I need some time to myself. I don't know what will happen after that."

"Whatever you do, just make sure it's what's best for you. I love you, Jess, and I hate it took you leaving me for me to see it."

"I love you too," I said as I leaned back against him.

Terminator had stopped next to the horse Decklan had been on, like he was telling Decklan to get the fuck off. Apparently, he got the hint when he slid off. "I think Terminator was dropping me off." He grabbed my hand. "Jess, you will always be special to me. I'll back off, but I will always be looking out to make sure you're good. If you ever need me, I'm a phone call away."

I slid off Terminator and hugged Decklan tightly. He kissed my forehead when I pulled away, and I lifted my head and kissed his lips. "Take care, Decklan."

He nodded. "You too, baby."

He mounted his horse and made his way back to the stable as I watched. Turning back to Terminator, I got back on. I pulled my phone from my bra again and checked Nate's message. *I hope you're having a great day. I hope to see you soon.*

I closed my eyes as my phone rang. When I saw Tyeis's number, I answered. "Hello?"

"Hey. I know we were supposed to be doing lunch in Beaumont today, but Decaurey just called, wanting to spend time with me."

"So you're dumping me. Is that what you're saying?" I asked, pretending to be offended.

"Hell yeah, bitch! I can go to lunch with yo' ass anytime."

"Well, I guess you won't be ready to leave by tomorrow morning."

"Aww. How did the talk go?"

"It went good. I'm just feeling a little sensitive, and I wanna go home now. I'll hang around until Tuesday morning like I promised."

"You don't have to do that. We can go tomorrow. If Decaurey wants to get to know me, he knows how to drive, and so do I. If you need to go home, then we're going home. I rode here with you," Ty said.

"Thank you for understanding."

"Of course. I'm your friend. Well, let me go so I can get ready. I'll talk to you when we get back."

"Okay. Have fun."

I ended the call and made my way back to the stable to stall Terminator. Once I did, I went to the back porch where my uncles were still seated, puffing cigars. As I got closer, Uncle Storm said, "Y'all shol looked friendly and shit. We came out here in case you needed back up."

"I appreciate y'all."

"A'ight. Just remember this shit when I need you for my campaign."

I rolled my eyes and asked, "How is Noni with the college-aged boyfriend?"

I asked that shit to take the attention off me. He rolled his eyes as Uncle Jasper chuckled. "She claims he's her friend's cousin and that they were just talking. Fuck that. I blocked his ass through my phone. He better find somebody else's daughter to befriend, 'cause mine ain't the one. And watch your face when I talk about my campaign."

"Uncle Storm! There are only four hundred people here now! You don't need a damn campaign!"

I laughed as he laughed sarcastically. "Bruh, I honestly think you're a shoe in for it," Uncle Marcus said as Uncle Jasper laughed.

"What the fuck is so funny, Jasper? You been laughing for the past hour," Uncle Storm said.

"Because you doing all this shit for nothing. Abney ain't running. Right now, you the only nigga wanting that damn job. Whether people vote for you or not, you gon' win if ain't nobody running against you."

I laughed so loud Aunt Tiffany had to come outside to see what was so funny. She looked around, waiting for someone to fill her in.

"Uncle Storm is the only one running for mayor. Abney isn't running again."

"So basically, the fucking Gabriel of Big City Nome spending all that damn money for nothing?"

Uncle Jasper nodded then took a puff of his cigar. As he exhaled, he said, "And one thing Storm hates is wasting money. That's a shame he wasted all that money."

"Fuck you, Jasper. I'm going home. You can walk to yours. Let's go, Marcus."

He stood from his seat and left Uncle Jasper. Uncle Jasper didn't live far from here anyway. Leave it to my family to get me out of the dumps. I sat next to Uncle Jasper, and he pulled out a cigar from his shirt pocket and handed it to me. "Let me find out you the fucking plug out here."

He almost got choked. "Shiiiid, I might as well be... for weed, anyway. I'm always stocked."

I shook my head then kissed his cheek. "Thanks, Unc."

CHAPTER SIXTEEN

BRIXTON

When I got back to Nome, I almost wished I could have stayed gone. I was no longer visiting. I was a citizen once again. What made it worse was that the love that I'd fucked up with family was here. I would always be reminded of her, not to mention I would probably see her whenever she came to town.

I couldn't focus on my issues with Jessica though. I needed to talk to my mama. She was of utmost importance right now. I knew she was feeling a way about everything that had happened, and I needed to mend our relationship ASAP. One thing life had taught me was that it wasn't promised. In the blink of an eye, I could lose her without warning. I would never forgive myself if something happened to her. Furthermore, death didn't have an age requirement. I could very well leave this earth before her.

It was time out for being petty and stubborn. Helen Lewis meant everything to me, and I needed her to know that. She was still grieving the loss of my father... the man she'd been married to for thirty-five years. I knew that was hard for her. It had been hard for me, which was why it was so easy for me to get angry.

I pulled in the driveway to see her outside on her knees. I

frowned slightly and got out of my truck to see she was planting something. Smiling slightly, I made my way to her. "Hey, Mama."

"Hey, baby. I'm glad you made it back safely."

Her voice sounded so weary. It only made me feel worse inside. "What are you planting?"

She glanced up at me and smiled. "Well, I've been out here all day. Over there are bell peppers, next to them are cucumbers, then onions. Right here, I'm planting tomatoes."

I gave her a tight smile then went to my knees to help her. I hadn't done this in a long time, but I hadn't forgotten. I sank my fingers in the dirt and began helping her plant. Gloves were never needed for a country nigga like me. I just always made sure to wash my hands really well afterward.

"Mama, I'm sorry."

"You don't owe me an apology, baby. I'm sorry for not telling you and Stacy about the mess we created."

"I realized when I was closing the gym that I was part of the problem. Before I locked the doors, I walked through the place. In my mind, I felt like a failure. My mind went to Dad, and I reminded myself of him. It's sad because I looked at my father as a failure. Whenever I have feelings of defeat, failure, or inadequacy, I think about him. My thoughts are all screwed up. My perception of who my father was as a man was all fucked up. Excuse my language, Mama."

She gently rubbed my back as I planted tomato seeds. "It's okay, baby."

I looked over at her when I heard her voice tremble and saw the tear fall down her cheek. I leaned my forehead against hers. "Y'all were doing the best that you could. Stacy and I were so selfish, we couldn't see that. Dad wasn't a failure. He never gave up. That man worked hard to provide for us. Sometimes he came up short, but none of us were hurt because of it. Y'all didn't come to me about the money because you knew how I would respond."

"Baby, we didn't want you or Stacy to have to be involved.

We'd made a mess of things by trying to do more than we could afford, in hopes that the return would be great. It never worked out. We only kept digging a deeper hole to bury us in. The stress of all that is what killed your father. He was trying so hard to be independent and not ask for help. It wasn't until he knew we were for sure going to lose the property that he asked for help. Our credit wasn't good enough to go to a bank. That was why we went to Mr. Jeffcoat."

"Still, Mama. It wasn't for me to condemn y'all. It took my business failing to realize that. Sometimes we aren't in control, and that's a hard pill to swallow. When the Hendersons showed up, I got angry. Like Dad, I was filled with pride, upset that they knew my business. I hated that. I blamed Jessica, saying that she'd told them what I told her in strict confidence. Then when I knew she hadn't said a word, I still blamed her for knowing about it and not telling me she knew. That was so stupid. Now she won't talk to me. I'm scared I may have lost her."

"Jessica is a lot like your grandmother was... my mother. She didn't take any mess. If she got mad, you had to give her three to five business days to cool down." She chuckled. "If you didn't, she'd unleash a fury on you that you'd never seen. However, once she cooled down, her heart always shined through. She needed time to get over whatever she was angry about. So give Jessica time."

"What if she doesn't come around?"

"Jessica loves you, baby. When I came home that day and y'all were in the recliner together, I could see it by the way she looked at you. Although she didn't want to admit it, I truly believed she loved you when y'all were in high school. So with time, I believe that she will reach out to you."

"Thanks, Mama."

I kissed her forehead and finished planting the seeds as a truck turned in the driveway. I noticed it was Kenny and his friend, Shylou. I went to the water hose at the side of the house and rinsed my hands then went back to where they were. "What's up, man?" Kenny asked.

"Not too much. Just finished planting tomatoes with my mama. What are y'all up to?"

"Well, we were brainstorming about a business venture for you, and Jessica came to mind. She loves horses. Shylou and I think you ought to open horse stables for boarding. A barn would be extremely simple to build."

Shylou glanced at him. "I don't know how simple it is. I just know that I can't build one, so it can't be that simple. But shit, if you build that and invest in a couple of horses, Jessica will love you long time," he said, mimicking a Chinese accent. "Plus... you ready for this?"

"What?"

"Noah wants to shoot a video with Jess right out here in the country. This will happen toward the end of the summer, so we're going to help you get these stables built. Noah would pay you a fee to use your facilities. The publicity alone will get you business you never dreamed of."

I glanced over at my mama, and she smiled at me. I closed my eyes for a moment and nodded. "Let's do it, but only if I can pay y'all back."

Kenny and Shylou stared at one another then both extended their hands to me for a handshake. I shook them both and said, "Thank y'all. I appreciate you coming up with something to make the farm some money to sustain itself."

"No problem, nephew," Kenny said with a smile.

I lowered my head. "You know she's not talking to me right now, right?"

"Mm hmm. But I also know you ain't giving up, right?"

I gave him a tight smile. "I'm not, but I know she needs time."

Shylou chuckled. "Don't give her ass too much time though. She doesn't have anything for a while since the shoot in Cali got postponed."

"I'm gonna try not to. She's not answering my calls or text messages, though, and I've never been to her place."

"Don't worry about that. I'll shoot you her address. We gotta go.

We'll be in touch about the stables. I think we should be able to start next month some time."

"Sounds like a plan. I appreciate all the love. Man, y'all have me speechless."

"That's what family does. Talk to you later, man," Kenny said as they went back to their truck.

I turned to my mama and said, "I guess all that debt did one thing: It got me involved in one of the most affluent and generous families in Jefferson County. Even though I messed up with Jess, they are still here for me."

Beaumont and all the surrounding areas knew about the Hendersons, especially for their rice, roux, and grass farms. Their products could be found in every store in Southeast Texas and Southwest Louisiana. W.J. was right. They were blessed because they blessed others... people like me.

"That's because they know a good man when they see one. You're a good man, Brixton. You want better for yourself and won't settle for mediocrity. They can see that in you, baby. I love you."

"Thanks. Mama. I love you too."

I pulled my phone from my pocket and sent Jessica a message. *Hey, baby. I'm not giving up on you. I love you so much. So prepare to get sick of me hitting you up. I won't stop until you force me to.*

CHAPTER SEVENTEEN

JESSICA

I rang the doorbell at Nate's place then adjusted my overnight bag on my shoulder. When the door opened, he was standing his tall ass there shirtless with a bouquet of roses. That took me by surprise, but I supposed it shouldn't have. He was thoughtful and sweet like that. I smiled brightly, genuinely happy to see him. It had been a rough few days. We ended up staying in Nome until Monday evening. I needed to make my rounds to see everyone before I left and ended up seeing Brixton pulling into his driveway.

When he noticed my car at Uncle Kenny's house, he tried to get my attention, but I kept right on driving. I was hoping he didn't follow me back to my mama's house, and he didn't. I was going there to pick up Tyeis and to tell my parents and Jacob goodbye one last time. I also had to check in on my grandmother. She seemed to be doing okay, but she wasn't her usually spunky self. I wasn't the only one who noticed.

All my aunts and uncles seemed worried about her health, as was Grandpa. She was extremely quiet when I spent time with her Sunday. She only talked when I asked her a question. Grandpa had taken her to the doctor, but they only found that her blood pressure was slightly elevated. They said that could occur with the summer cold she had, especially at her age. They said if her condition didn't improve, to take her to the hospital to be evaluated.

Nate allowed me to walk inside his home, and it was gorgeous. It looked to be a two-story home from the outside and was a somewhat open floorplan on the inside. As I walked further inside, I turned to him, and he extended the flowers. "Jess, you look amazing as always."

"So do you, Nate," I responded, glancing down at his lean but defined chest. "You have a beautiful home."

"Thank you."

I took the flowers from him and sniffed them as he took my purse and bag and set them on the couch. "Come to the kitchen. My chef made dinner for us."

I smiled and followed him to the massive kitchen. My mama and Aunt Chrissy would be in hog heaven in here. It was extremely spacious. There were two sink areas, four huge ovens, two microwaves, a fancy ass refrigerator, and a huge cooktop. "My mama would have a field day if she had a kitchen this size in her home. She'd never stay out of it."

He smiled and led me to a bar stool. He helped me up to be seated then kissed my forehead. "I'm so happy you're here. When the season is done, your mom is welcome to come cook in here anytime."

I smiled again as I watched him get the food from the oven. My mind seemed clear for the moment. I'd taken today to get reacquainted with myself. I pampered myself all day long. I went to a spa and got a massage, facial, wax, a mani/pedi, and got my hair done. The day was peaceful. While I was mentally trying to convince myself that I was doing what was best for me by ignoring Brix, I knew that I would have to talk to him eventually, like I did to Decklan, to truly be at peace with how things turned out.

After exercising, I soaked in my tub in lavender oils and crystals until I damn near fell asleep. However, when I got out and had moisturized my skin and got dressed, I felt good. I'd even gathered the nerve to schedule an appointment with a psychiatrist. I would be seeing her Friday evening before I headed to Dallas for the weekend. I'd told Nate that I would love to spend the weekend with him.

He'd bought me a plane ticket to meet him there Friday night, and he said he had lavish plans for us Saturday. I was really looking forward to it. There had been no talks of us being together. Nate was just going with the flow of things. In a short time, he knew me well. We'd established a friendship, although it started off in a different direction. He wasn't the one who'd taken it there though. That was all me. I had a feeling that things would be different tonight.

He set a plate of seafood pasta in front of me, and my mouth watered. It smelled so good, and I loved alfredo sauce. This only added to his points with me. He hadn't done a thing to offend me in any way, and he was cautious about how he approached me and spoke to me. It wasn't in a nervous sort of way but one of total consideration. The man was perfect so far, and that spoke volumes to me.

"This looks really good."

"Yeah. Chef G. Garvin doesn't miss."

"G. Garvin?" I asked as my eyebrows lifted.

"Mm hmm. He was in town and did me a solid after I promised him two tickets to the game in Dallas tomorrow. We talked about him before, and you said how good his food looked. So I wanted you to find out how good it tasted too."

"Damn, Nate. That's so sweet. Thank you."

He sat next to me and grabbed my hand to say grace, but I stopped him by putting my hands to his face, pulling it to mine, to offer him a tender kiss on the lips. When I pulled away, his eyes remained closed as he hummed softly. "I'll get that nigga to cook for you every day if I'm gon' get to taste those sweet lips as a thank you gift."

I smiled as I wrapped my arms around his neck. "This is perfect."

Everything from the top of his braided head to the sole of his size eighteen feet was perfect. I knew his feet were huge when I saw those boats. It was one of the first questions I asked him when we established a friendship. He'd laughed and said he could tell I'd been dying to ask that question. We'd laughed about it for a few minutes before we could move on to a different topic of discussion.

"Get to your food before it gets cold, baby. We can do this for the rest of the evening. Plus, you smell so damn good I'm getting distracted. You can make me lose focus on everything else." He stroked my cheek. "You're so beautiful, Jess... inside and out."

I smiled as my cheeks heated up while I stared at him. "And you're handsome as hell."

He smiled back and kissed me again. The kiss started to get more involved as I held him tightly. I slid my tongue to his, and he moaned into my mouth before pulling away. "See what you starting... food. Eat."

I laughed and so did he as he grabbed my fork and started to feed me. I closed my eyes and savored the flavor. This food tasted even better than it looked. "Mm. Nate, that man's palate is blessed. This food is so good. You are the real MVP for getting him to cater this meal. Damn."

He gave me a one-cheeked smile and fed me more. I picked up his fork and fed him as well. He did the same as me, closing his eyes and moaning, mocking my response to G. Garvin's food, making me laugh. I playfully swatted him and began feeding myself. "So, we didn't talk about how the talk with your mom went," I said.

"That's because we didn't have one. I don't think I'm ready. Too much anger about the situation is still inside of me. I need to give myself time to calm down about it and maybe see it from her perspective better. Otherwise, I'll probably disrespect her in some way. Then I won't be able to live with myself afterward."

I nodded repeatedly as I gave him a tight smile. "I totally understand. By the time I talked to my mom, I'd worked through it on my own. I guess I've always been that way too. I see we have that in common. No matter how angry we feel or how wrong we think we've been done, we still consider our loved ones' feelings before our own, especially our mothers. I believe that practice can be good and bad.

However, in this instance, I think it's a good thing. Have you talked to Noah since the game?"

"Yeah. We talk often... maybe every other day."

We continued eating in silence until Nate asked, "You want something a little stronger to drink? I'm about to pour some Hennessy."

"Yeah. I'll take a lil bit. Thank you."

I ate the rest of my food in silence. Even after Nate came back with my drink, I thanked him and went back to my food. He killed his, too, then sipped his drink. After putting our dishes away, he came back to me and helped me off the stool. I could tell the alcohol had him feeling nice. He looked slightly tipsy. The way he caressed my curves with his eyes didn't go unnoticed though. It would take more than one glass of alcohol for me to lose my inhibitions, though, if I wasn't comfortable. That let me know he didn't drink often. He was a lightweight.

When we sat, I slipped off my sandals and tucked my feet under me. I leaned into him as he put his arm around me. This felt good, but for the first time tonight, Brix entered my mind. I closed my eyes, wondering what he was doing and how he was feeling. I missed him. *He got you fucked up though, Jess. You accept that type of behavior, you'll always be accepting it. He needs to know that it's not acceptable.*

"You good, baby? You quiet," Nate asked as he lifted my head by my chin.

"Yeah. What about you?"

"Mm hmm. Any time in your presence is a good time."

He kissed my lips, and I thought I saw God. The man was gifted in so many ways. He knew I would deepen this Hennessy flavored kiss. Before I even realized it, I was lying on the couch, and he was on top of me. *Jessica, what in the fuck are you doing?* My mind was wearing me out about moving too quickly, but I ignored it and kept going. When his hand went under my shirt and pulled my nipple from my bra, my eyes rolled to the back of my head.

I pulled at my shirt, giving him permission to pull it off. He did so quickly and unfastened my bra. When his tongue graced my nipple, my clit hardened, and I could practically feel that shit rubbing against my panties. I grabbed his head as he flicked my nipple back and forth with his tongue. "Oh fuck, Nate. You gon' make me cum."

He lifted his head and began pulling at my pants. I gladly lifted my hips, and he pulled them, along with my underwear, off in record speed. I was glad he wasn't being so tender now. I didn't need to be in my feelings. This would be a fuck, and I could possibly move on from here like normal. Once my pants were off, he went to my pussy and pushed my legs open wider. I had a moment of déjà vu, remembering the night of the trail ride party over four months ago.

Nate's mouth covered my clit, and I couldn't handle it. He was sucking it so good he made me wonder what I needed my rose vibrator for. My hands traveled to his ears, and I held on for dear life as my orgasm ripped through me like a fucking tornado. "Nate! Fuck!"

I refused to leave him hanging this time. My mind was still on Brix, and no matter how hard I tried to swallow thoughts of him, they kept coming back up. My soul was telling me to stop again, but Nate would never forgive me for this shit. He lifted his head, and I pulled him to me. His body slid on top of mine, and I sucked my taste from his lips. "That's some good shit, huh?" he asked in a low voice.

"Yeah, but I'm sure you have some good shit too. Let me taste it, Nate."

He went to his knees on the couch as he stared at me. It was like he was expecting me to stop him again. The intensity of his stare was too much for me. I grabbed my nipples and closed my eyes. It felt like he was x-raying my fucking insides, knowing that I was covering up something. When I reopened my eyes, he was standing in front of me in all his naked glory.

This man was so fucking fine. He was hung like a damn mule, and if I wanted it, it could be all mine. I felt that in my soul. Nate wanted me to be his exclusively. I'd known for a while. Was I giving him false hope? Instead of dwelling on that, I sat up and pulled his dick into my mouth. His ass was so tall, his dick was right in my face without me having to lean over to get to it.

When my mouth covered what I could, I put my hand around the base and began stroking him at the same pace I was sucking him. Nate didn't have a size eighteen foot for nothing. His dick looked to be a foot long. I was nervous as hell, knowing I wouldn't be able to take all this shit. I may not have been lucky in love, but shit if I wasn't lucky with dick. Decklan, Brix, and Nate were hung like the stars in the sky. *Brixton.*

I closed my eyes and shook my head, trying to rid myself of thoughts of Brixton. All that did was cause Nate to bust in my mouth. "Shit!" he yelled. "I'm sorry, Jess. I didn't ask if that was cool. That shit snuck up on me."

I allowed some of his nut to run down my chin, then I stuck out my tongue and licked it back up. I massaged what fell to my breasts in my skin as he watched and leaked more. I pulled him back into my mouth and sucked the residuals out of him as his body trembled. "Jessica, fuck! Yeah, baby," he said as he grabbed my head and began slow fucking my mouth.

He pulled out of my mouth and just stared at me. To convince him I wasn't backing out this time, I leaned back on the couch and spread my legs then began playing with my pussy. When I brought my fingers to my mouth, he dropped to his knees and rubbed the head of his dick up my slit, covering it with my juices, then stood and brought it back to my mouth. I sucked him clean, then he left me on the couch for a moment.

I assumed he went to get a condom. It was like he was in shock that it was actually going down this time. I was in shock, too, but I knew I was too far gone to change my mind now. I cared about Nate. By the time he came back, he was strapped up and had another in his hand. He immediately went to his knees and pushed inside of me, taking my fucking breath right out of my body. It seemed his breathing went on hiatus too. He allowed his dick to just sit there for a few seconds. The goosebumps had covered his skin and mine. "Fuck!" he yelled.

When he began stroking me, I creamed and squirted every fucking where. "Naaaaate! Shiiit!" I screamed.

He stroked me faster, giving me just what I didn't know I needed. I knew he wasn't giving me all of it, because there was no way my pussy could take everything he had to offer. However, I knew I could take more than what he was giving me. "Give me more, Nate. Slowly give me more, baby."

He bit his bottom lip and leaned over me, pushing more inside of me and stroking me slowly. "Oh my God. I'm about to cum again, Nate."

He was quiet as fuck as he stared at me... exploring the depths of my soul. I closed my eyes because he was fucking up my nut. He gave me more until I pressed my hand against his chest. He began stroking me again, and I came without warning, just as he had. "Jess, this some good shit, girl. I'm about to nut. Fuck!"

My eyes remained closed as I panted, soaking in the realization of what had just happened. I didn't regret this, because it was good as fuck, but I also realized at this moment, Nate wasn't the man I was supposed to be with. Even with as good as sex was with him, my heart didn't feel it, and I believed he sensed it.

He pulled out of me, and when I opened my eyes, he was staring at me as he strapped up again. I held his stare, and he gave me a tight smile. He lowered his head for a moment then looked back up at me. "Once more, baby. I know this will probably be the last time, so let me make love to you."

I nodded as I swallowed hard and lay back against the couch cushions. Nate pushed his dick inside of me slowly and stared into my eyes like he was pleading with me to say that he was wrong... that we would be a couple and engage in these types of activities all the time. I couldn't. I didn't know how he could tell, but I was glad that he could, because that meant I didn't have to say it.

His dick touched every crevice of my pussy and had me cumming the Nile. I knew his sofa would need cleaning after this shit. He loved me. No man could make love to me and make me actually feel that shit unless he loved me. I stared into his eyes as the tears sprang from mine and a soft cry left my lips. "I'm so sorry, Nate."

He bit his bottom lip and was about to pull away from me. I stopped him. "Please don't stop. I can feel how much you love me. Please don't stop."

He leaned over and kissed my lips as he continued to stroke me passionately. I had to be a fool. How would I let him go? Couldn't I eventually fall for him as he had fallen for me? When he separated the kiss, he went to my neck and shoulder. "Damn, Jess. I fell in love wit'chu, girl. Fuck. What am I supposed to do now, baby?"

His strokes became stronger as my cries became louder. My nails dug into his flesh as he gave me every ounce of love inside of him. Listening to his moans and words of desperation had me crying like a baby but cumming at the same time. I was overwhelmed emotionally, and I didn't know what to do with myself. "Jess, I'm trying to make this shit last. I don't want to let go, baby. Shit."

I pushed him away from me and stood from the couch. I gestured for him to sit, and I straddled him, sliding down his dick at the same time. I couldn't go all the way down, but I took most of it. I stared at him as the tears continued to escape me and began riding him at a slow pace, trying to make his wish come true and make this shit last.

"Nate, please don't ever forget me. I care for you so much. This is hard, and it hurts. I don't want to let go either, but it won't be fair to you for me to keep holding on if I don't feel the same way you do."

He grabbed my ass without responding to me and assisted my ride. I stared at him, but he started to do as I did earlier. He wouldn't return my gaze. I grabbed his face and turned it to mine and kissed his lips until he came in the latex. He held me close for a while, resting his head against mine. "I love you, Jess. I could never forget you, baby. Promise me that if what you want doesn't want you back that you would give me another chance."

"I promise, Nate."

He held me tight as I relaxed against him, wishing things were different. However, I knew that my heart belonged to Brix. Until we could get that shit straight, or I could get my heart back, I needed to remain single and find my way back to myself before involving anyone else in my bullshit.

CHAPTER EIGHTEEN

BRIXTON

It had been three weeks since I'd seen or heard from Jess, and I refused to take this separation lying down. I had to fight for her. That was why I was on my way to Houston. I fucked up, but was what I did so unforgiveable? In my eyes, it wasn't, but unfortunately, my eyes didn't matter. The only eyes that mattered at this point were hers. I just hoped she could find it in her heart to forgive me for being an insensitive, proud jackass.

I'd been regrouping and trying to come up with a business proposal to present to a local bank. Although we'd discussed the stables, I knew it wouldn't generate steady income at first. So Kenny and I had done some serious brainstorming, and he suggested that I just open a gym in Nome. He said people all around here went to Beaumont to workout. So we came up with the idea for a gym and a hike and bike trail. Of course, I wouldn't charge for the hike and bike trail, but I could include it in the proposal.

Kenny had looked over everything for me, and Jasper's wife, Chasity, had gone over the numbers. The Hendersons had stepped up for me in major ways. Whatever I could do to help them in the future would be a done deal, no questions asked. They'd stepped up for me in ways I couldn't believe. Even when I went to the bank, Kenny and Jasper accompanied me. It was almost guaranteed I would get this loan from their presence alone. They'd even said they would cosign if I needed it.

I couldn't believe they would step up for me that way. No one had ever done something of that magnitude for me. Hell, I didn't know anyone that *could* do something like that for anybody! I was blessed, and I knew my connection to Jessica had something to do with that. Before I left, I talked to Kenny and told him that I was going to Houston and to wish me luck.

Since Decaurey had been talking to Tyeis, Jakari had gotten the entail from him about Jessica's schedule. Tyeis had said that Jess had been on break for nearly two weeks. That was shocking to me, because she'd told me that she normally went to Nome when she had long breaks like that. I supposed since I was there and Nesha was married, she wasn't in a hurry to get there.

I was about twenty minutes from her condo, and I was nervous as fuck. I didn't know how she would react to me popping up on her. It would probably be like déjà vu for her, reminding her of Decklan. Kenny said that she and Decklan had talked a day or two before she left. He was the one who encouraged me to go to her. Although I'd said I would hunt her ass down if I had to, my reservations with the situation had crept in.

All the things I'd said about Decklan seemed to be true for me as well. I'd been texting and calling her every day, probably stressing her the fuck out. However, like him, I wouldn't give up until she talked to me and told me to leave her the fuck alone. Otherwise, I would continue harassing her. Jessica was supposed to be mine. We were destined, and I could feel it. I knew she could too. I just had to prove to her that I wasn't the man that verbally attacked her for something she had nothing to do with... not knowingly anyway.

When I got to her place and saw her car, my heart rate picked up a bit. I'd never been nervous about approaching a woman. Well, it wasn't me approaching her that had me nervous. It was what her response would be that had me about to sweat. I didn't want to continue life without her. She was the woman I needed more than anyone else. She was my soulmate. I had to fix this shit, even if it wasn't an easy fix.

I got out and made my way to the door. The moisture in my beard caught me off guard. I needed to chill out. After ringing the doorbell, I took a step back to see if I saw any movement inside. It looked pretty dark. I rang it again then turned to look around, only to bump right into Jess. "You looking for me?" she asked seriously.

"Yeah, hey," I said as I scanned her sweaty body clad in spandex. "I just got here," I said.

I couldn't keep my eyes off her sexy ass body. She nodded then reached in her fanny pack. "I'm assuming you want to talk. Let me take a shower first."

"Okay."

She opened the door and said, "Make yourself comfortable. Give me about thirty minutes."

I nodded and watched her ass jiggle as she walked away. *Damn.* She was so fucking fine. I went to the couch and chilled out while she took a shower. She seemed so nonchalant, like my presence didn't rock her world. I could tell she was just as nervous as I was. I could see her body tremble as she spoke. She was a sweaty mess, but that only made her sexier. Her stepdad was right on the money when he asked her to be a model for his boutique. Her humble beginnings had become a thing of the past. I saw her on a billboard for Ashley Stewart on my way here.

I played on my phone, trying not to stress too much about what I thought she might say. As I played on my phone, I saw I had an email from the bank. I quickly opened it to see I had gotten the loan! I was too excited. I digitally signed those papers she sent over so damn fast I could barely see straight. I texted Kenny immediately.

I got the loan! Thank you so much for all you've done to help me.
No problem. Congratulations. You made it to Houston yet?

Yes. I'm waiting for her to get cleaned up. She'd just gotten back from working out. I'm nervous as hell, but I didn't come all the way out here to leave without her being in my life.

Man up and get what you went there for. I'm proud of you. It's important to rectify your mistakes. I feel like she's going to eventually let you do that. If she doesn't give in this time, don't give up. You'll wear her down.

I smiled slightly as I read his last message. He was her family, so he knew her better than me. According to him, she was a mixture of her mother and her aunt Tiffany. She was hard on the outside, but once a person passed that hard shell, she was soft as cotton. I knew that to be true. I'd seen it that night she got high. When I heard a door close, I stood to see her coming down the hallway. She had on some tight shorts and a T-shirt and had her hair wrapped in a towel.

"You want anything to drink?" she asked as she went to the kitchen.

"No, I'm good. Thanks."

"Mm hmm," she said as I watched her pull a bottle of Patrón from the cabinet. She poured some in a small glass then made her way to the couch. Once she sat, I sat as well. "How are you, Jess?"

"I'm okay. How about you?"

"Missing you. I'm sorry for popping up on you. I just couldn't go another day of you ignoring my texts and calls. I know that shit is on me, but I want to make things right between us."

"Why?"

"Because I love you, Jess. You're the woman that's been in my soul for the past fifteen years. I need you."

"A wise person once told me, if they don't do right by you, maybe it's because they *don't* love you. So why should I believe you love me since you were so quick to accuse me of talking your business to my family? I guess you thought I was down there begging them to have mercy on the little poor boy."

She'd thrown my words right back in my face, as I knew her petty ass would. "I'm not a wise person, Jess. If I were, I wouldn't have talked to you crazy."

"You fucking right about that shit. You lucky you got away with that."

"Jess, just please tell me that I still have a chance at your heart. Tell me that I didn't fuck everything up."

She stood and gulped the rest of her drink then went back to the kitchen, leaving me on ice. I was trembling and shit like a fucking fiend, waiting for her to come back. She took her fucking time too. After five minutes or longer, she sat back in the seat she once occupied. When she smiled slightly, I hopped up from my seat and pulled her from hers, wrapping my arms around her.

That small gesture let me know that she wasn't giving up on us. She slid her arms around me and said, "I missed you, Brix."

"Damn, baby. I'm so sorry for how I spoke to you. I can imagine that it took you to painful times in your life."

"It did. That's why I had to block out the world. I've been taking care of me. While I know how to handle it and work through it, I don't want to keep being triggered. I want to have so much peace until it's impossible for me to be triggered. I went to see a psychiatrist, and she helped me with some techniques I can use to come out of that mindset. It won't happen overnight, but if I make a conscious effort to focus on the positive aspects of my life, it will become habit."

"Damn. What made you forgive me, Jess? I was fully prepared to chase your ass like Decklan was doing. I had my stalker paperwork submitted and everything."

"I forgave you a while ago," she said, totally ignoring my weak ass joke.

"Well, what made you still want to be with me?"

"I couldn't stop thinking about you. It didn't help you were calling and texting every day. There were some other factors that convinced me that I would rather not talk about as well. What's important is that I want to be with you, despite yo' ignorant ass talking to me like a jackass."

"You right. I'm sorry again, baby. I promise that shit will never happen again."

"It better not. I don't give second chances. That shit is unheard of. So if it happens again, I'm gon' let Jasper use you for bait when he's hunting for those wild hogs. They'll eat your ass without leaving a trace. Won't even be able to find any hair. Who broke code and gave you my address?"

"Kenny."

"Wait until I tell Uncle Storm."

"That nigga too busy trying to get his team together for when he takes office."

She laughed, and I swore it was the sweetest sound I'd heard since she'd been gone. It was a sound I never thought I would hear again. I was definitely curious about what her other reasons were for giving me a second chance. For some reason, I felt that Nate had a lot to do with that. "I'd planned to make a trip to Nome this coming weekend to see my family, and I was going to talk to you as well."

"Really? Why?"

"I was going to let you know that I forgave you. If you didn't bite, I wasn't going to make the first move. I would have gone on through life without you. However, because of all your text messages and calls, I was pretty certain that you would do just what you did today."

I lowered my head. "And what is it that I'm doing today?"

"Begging. Some Keith Sweat 'Make It Last Forever' kind of begging."

I chuckled. "You're worth every note his begging ass sang."

She giggled. I brought my hand to her face and gently stroked her cheek then leaned in, waiting for her to tell me to move or stop. When she didn't, I was happy as shit. I laid my lips on hers and relished the feeling of her soft lips being on mine. Jessica was the woman I loved, and I refused to give up on her. This moment made me grateful that I didn't. When I tried to pull away, she held my face to hers as she slowly kissed me.

After pulling away from me, she asked, "Are you staying the night?"

"Do you want me to?"

"Well, yeah. You have plenty of making up to do, so I figured you would want to get a head start. But if not, I mean, I totally understand."

"Hell yeah, I want to spend the night. I was hoping you would ask."

"Good. Well, the shower is obviously available. I'm gonna go pull my hair up."

She walked away as I watched her make her way down the hallway. That woman was going to be the death of me. God definitely had a sense of humor. I thought I was coming here to get on my knees and beg her to be mine, only for her to make this debacle as painless as possible. Once she disappeared, I took the moment to thank God for favor, His grace and mercy. He'd softened her heart just for me.

I pulled out my phone then stood to go to the shower. I messaged Kenny. *Everything went great. Thanks, man.*

I knew it would. See you when you get back.

I smiled as I made my way down the hallway. When I saw the bathroom door open with the light on, I went inside so I could start the shower then go outside to get my bag. Jess was in the mirror pulling her hair into a ponytail. She smiled at me. "So what did you decide to do about your business?"

"I closed the gym and put it for sale. There have been a couple of potential buyers. I've had all my things moved into a storage in Beaumont, and I sold my house. They are supposed to be closing on it next week. Depending on what the gym sells for, I may have to get the equipment out of it. That would save me a lot of money, since I will be building a gym in Nome."

Her eyes widened. "Really? That's great!"

"Yeah, it is. Your uncles went to the bank with me, and while you were showering, I read an email saying that I'd been approved for a million-dollar loan. I won't need all of it. Once the gym in Austin sells, I'll apply that to the loan. That Henderson name carries weight. Thank you for wanting what was best for me, baby. Thank you for introducing me to your family. They've been a blessing to me and my mama. And a huge congratulations to you on landing a video with Noah! You about to blow up!"

Jessica blushed and giggled as she washed her hands. When she stared up at me again, she said, "Thank you! Congratulations to you too, Brix, and you're welcome."

She turned away, and I could tell she was taking deep breaths. "You good?"

She nodded and smiled slightly. I brushed my fingertips across her cheek. "I'm gonna go get my bag from the car. I'll be right back."

"Okay."

I left the bathroom, trying to figure out what was bothering her that quickly. She almost looked like she was on the verge of an anxiety attack. I quickly made my way to my car and hurried back, just in case something was indeed wrong with her. When I got back inside, I locked the door and practically power walked to the bathroom. I walked inside to find Jess naked as the day she was born. "Damn, baby. What'chu doing? You showering with me?"

She shook her head. "I'm waiting for you to get out, so hurry."

She slid her hand across my cheek as she walked out. That was when I noticed she had heels on. I bit my bottom lip as I peeked out of the bathroom to see her walking up the stairs. *Fuck!* She didn't have to worry about me taking too long. Watching her beautiful body going up those stairs was luring me to her. The way her ponytail slid side to side across her back had me in a trance.

Breaking me from it, she said, "You're wasting time that you could be making love to all this body, Brix."

I blinked rapidly then licked my lips. Taking one last look, I went back inside the bathroom, showering in record time. Within fifteen minutes, I was done. That included washing my dick and pelvic area at least three times and moisturizing my body. I grabbed my bag and headed up the stairs in search of her.

Glancing in a couple of rooms as I passed them, I finally found her in the third one, sprawled out on the bed, her legs wide open, and her rose toy on her clit. I dropped my bag to the floor and got to her at the speed of light. I snatched the rose from her. "You starting without me?"

"Just getting warmed up."

"Let me warm you up, Jess. That's my job. This is an alternative for when we wanna play or I'm not here."

I tossed it to the bed and slid over her body. I closed my eyes, not believing that I was given this chance to prove to her all the things I told her... all the ways I planned to love her. She slid her hands up my chest to my shoulders, then to my face. She again took a deep breath as I hovered over her. I frowned slightly.

"Don't worry, Brix. I'm just trying to gather the nerve to say what I need to say to you."

"Damn. It's that serious?"

"Yeah. You know I've always been so closed off regarding my feelings, but for the past three weeks, I've been working on myself. Don't be alarmed, but Nate and I talked. I saw him when I left Nome. Somehow, he could tell that I was feeling someone else... thinking about someone else. That was when I knew how serious my feelings were for you. Nate was wining and dining me, being romantic as hell, and my mind was on you. I'm so scared of being hurt until it has had me crippled in my love life. I feel like all this time, I've been manifesting hurt."

That was deep what she said. We did that shit by giving it too much power. Half the time, we didn't even realize we were doing it. I maintained my position, hovering over her, as she turned her head away from me. I gently grabbed her chin and turned her back to me. "Keep going, Jess."

She swallowed hard and nodded. "I'm always anticipating being hurt, so I keep my wall up and keep my true feelings to myself. I don't want to do that shit anymore, Brix. I don't want to be shut off from the world. I want you to know that I love you, Brix. I'm in love with you, and I want to be all yours," she said as she stroked my beard.

I slid right into her paradise without a second thought. My eyes rolled to the back of my head as I allowed my heart to soak up her admission. "Jess, I love you too, and I plan to spend the rest of my life making sure you feel it."

I lifted her leg to my waist and stared into her slanted eyes as I made love to her, glad that she was finally mine.

EPILOGUE
JESSICA

Three months later...

"As the mayor of Big City Nome, Texas, I want to declare today as Phillip 'Vegas' Turner Day, where we all promise Jordans to kids and never give them to them."

Everybody chuckled. "Storm, you ain't even been elected yet! Election day is three months away!" Uncle Jasper said.

"Jasper, you gon' be the first person I abuse my power on. Ain't nobody running against me! Abney hadn't been serving in his office because he's been sick. I was serving in his spot! So nigga, from now on, you address me as Mr. Mayor! The fuck you on."

I lowered my head and slowly shook it. This nigga was gonna be a whole problem. They were gonna kick his ass out of office before he even got there. "As I was saying, may Vegas rest in peace. The streets of Nome won't be the same without him."

We were at the Henderson barn, turning up as usual, until Uncle Storm interrupted the festivities with his bullshit. Uncle Marcus nodded in agreement since he was 'working' in office with Uncle

Storm. They were gonna have a hot head and an ex-thug running Nome. This shit was gonna be a disaster.

Brixton sat next to me and put his arm around me. "Uncle Kenny invited us to dinner Sunday after church."

"Okay."

Brix, Uncle Kenny, and Uncle Jasper had gotten close. I was sure he and Lennox would become close before long, too, the more we hung out with them. We'd been going strong for the past three months. His gym was almost complete, and we'd broken ground on building a house. I couldn't believe I was doing this shit with just a boyfriend. I'd always said I wouldn't enter into agreements like that unless I was married. Brixton changed all that shit.

His gym had sold for nearly four hundred grand, and he was able to take the equipment as he'd hoped. He applied that money toward his loan. The stables were all done as well, and he had a steady stream of customers utilizing his services. The video shoot with Noah was next month, and I was beyond ready to introduce Brix to the country.

In the meantime, I was still living in Houston, and Brix was still living with his mother. I couldn't wait until we had better living arrangements. He spent one day a week in Houston, and I spent the weekends in Nome, if I wasn't working.

I found myself saying no to some offers now, just so I didn't have to work so hard. That was where I messed up last time. I was so caught up with being independent, I didn't make room for anything or anyone else. My independence was building an even taller wall around me, pushing everyone on the outside.

I'd spoken to Nate a couple of times to see how he was doing. He was having a hard time and had been allowing the memories Noah flooded his mind with to make him bitter toward his mother. The more Noah told him, the more he resented her. He felt like he missed out on so much, and I could understand how he felt. I told him to take a break from Noah's memories of David and just live in his truth. He needed to come to terms with the way things were. He promised me he would do that.

Decklan and I were on speaking terms as well. I could be around him without feeling a way. So whenever he decided to come to town to visit Lennox, we'd speak and even hug and keep it pushing. It was a blessing that Brixton wasn't a jealous person. He'd said, *"If anybody can take you from me with me doing everything right, they can have you. I know I'm the shit."*

I chuckled and shook my head when he said that. He and Decklan actually shook hands whenever they saw one another and were on speaking terms. He hadn't had to see Nate, and I didn't think he ever would. However, if he did, I knew it wouldn't be a problem. I'd found the right one this time. I could feel it in my heart. I no longer had to wonder where love was. It was right here at home. The place that had held the most memories of hurt for me, still held my future.

"Your uncle needs to sit his ass down," Nesha said as she sat on the other side of me.

"I dare you to go tell him."

"Hell no. So he can do me like he did Andrea at my wedding? No thank you."

I laughed, thinking about how I set that woman up. That was what she got for talking about my family. Nobody fucked with the Hendersons without consequence. "Aston, I told you that pets had to stay outdoors today, especially that rowdy ass cougar you got."

I laughed so loud. Vida cut her eyes at me and shot Uncle Storm the finger. Those two were always into it. Vida was Aunt Syn's mama, and she was over fifteen years older than her husband. As I turned my attention back to Nesha, she smiled at me. I didn't know what that smile was about, but I smiled back at her as Uncle Storm said, "Come on, Nesha. Don't take long, because I have some other shit to address."

Nesha rolled her eyes as she stood and went to the microphone.

Lennox joined her as she said, "Hey, everybody. I just wanted y'all to know that we're pregnant with the first Henderson great grandchild."

Applause went up, but I noticed Jakari didn't seem all that excited. I frowned slightly, then stood and went to him as Decaurey and Tyeis walked in. This was the first time they'd spent together since she'd come to town with me nearly four months ago. They seemed to be feeling one another, but she said they were taking it slow. She traveled just as much as I did, so their get to know you process was taking longer than normal.

I sat next to Jakari and grabbed his hand. My cousin was always happy. There was only one time when he wasn't and that was when they found out about his punk ass daddy raping Aunt Syn and Nesha when they were little girls. "J, you okay? You look upset about something."

He turned to me and slid his hand over his face. "She may not have the first Henderson great grandchild. This chick that was my lil dip told me she's six months pregnant. I haven't seen her in three months, so of course I hadn't noticed that she was pregnant. I was there for one thing and one thing only. I fucked up somewhere, but I don't remember fucking her without a condom. Seems like I would remember some shit like that, right?"

"Yeah, seems like you would," I said, totally invested in what he was saying to me.

"Jessica Shawntel Monroe."

I turned to the sound of my name being called with a frown on my face. When I saw Brix at the microphone, my eyebrows lifted. *What the fuck was he doing up there?* "Come here, baby," he said.

My heart jumped in my fucking throat as everyone stared at me with huge smiles on their faces. When I got to him, he smiled. "I just wanted to publicly thank you for giving me a second chance to prove my love to you. Since everyone here knows of the challenges we had because of me being too proud, I figured I could say this in front of them. I wanted them to know how much I love you and how I promise to be everything you need me to be."

That muthafucka pulled a box from his pocket and went to his knee. The tears fell from my eyes immediately as everyone screamed. I had a feeling this was what he was going to do, but his first statement had thrown me off somewhat. Everyone was screaming and applauding while Uncle Storm impatiently looked on.

"Jess, we have a lot of history. We've known one another since grade school and have been close friends since middle school. I always knew that I wanted you. Now that the time has come, I'm overwhelmed with joy. I want to make sure that this moment of our love is solidified by this ring. I love you so much, and I would be honored if you would be my wife."

I smiled at him as I swiped at tears. "Yes, Brix. Yes."

He slid the diamond ring on my finger then stood and scooped me up in his arms. For the moment, no one else was here—just him, me, and our love. I'd never been so happy in all my life, and I knew things would get even better.

"Jess, did you like my distraction?"

I turned to see Jakari standing there with a huge smile on his face. I hopped out of Brix's arms as I frowned. "Distraction? Your ass was lying?"

"Mm hmm. You was so deep in my business, you never saw Brix walk to the mic. Nesha will have the oldest great grandchild."

"I'ma fuck you up!"

Before I could grab him, Brix slid his arm around my waist and kissed my neck. "Not before you fuck me up though."

I turned and smiled at him as I noticed my aunts rubbing Nesha's belly. "You damn right, baby."

My mama appeared in front of me and hugged me tightly, along with Daddy and my brothers. "Congratulations, Jess," Jacob said. "You'll be a good wife, because you are a great big sister. I wish you all the happiness in the world. You deserve it."

"Don't start that shit and make me cry again! Thanks, brother. I love you."

I hugged CJ and Daddy then stared at my mama. The tears were falling down her face as she smiled. "I'm so grateful that God blessed you to find what you were searching for, baby. Congratulations."

"Thanks, Mama," I said as she pulled away from me and grabbed Brix's hand.

"There's no doubt in my mind that you will take care of my baby. Thank you for being good to her, Brixton."

"Thank you, Mrs. Jenahra."

After hugging a few more people, Uncle Storm picked me up and spun around with me. "Daddy, do me!" Remington yelled.

Uncle Storm rolled his eyes. "Can't do shit in front of him."

I chuckled as he wiped my tears with his thumb. "You and Nesha were like my little sisters instead of my nieces. To see y'all getting married is crazy. Congratulations. Don't have no long ass wedding like your cousin though."

"Her wedding wasn't that long. You're just impatient. You gon' have to work on that, Mayor."

He smiled as he nodded repeatedly. I could see calling him that would butter his ass up enough to make biscuits. He shook Brix's hand without even responding to what I'd said. When he walked away, Brix pulled me in his arms. "It was a journey, but we made it," he said.

"Hell yeah. We made it back to love."

The End

If you did not read the author's note at the beginning, please go back and do so before leaving a review. 😊

FROM THE AUTHOR...

Listen... Jessica was a whole movement by herself. She represented so many of us that pretend to be unbothered but cry in the privacy of our homes. Her 'make it look easy' demeanor was inspired by the song of the same title by Chlöe. She played hard in front of everybody until she broke... or got high. LOL! Her trauma and hurt from her father were deep, and I felt sorry for her. She pulled herself through that ordeal and healed from it the best way she knew how.

Brixton was a traditional man. He reminded me of Lem in the movie, *Soul Food*, when it came to getting help from his woman. While Jessica didn't go to her ex to help him, he thought she'd gone to her family. He was too proud for his own good. Thankfully, he saw the error of his ways. He was dealing with a lot, and he too represents a lot of people. When we're under pressure, we lash out on those that are there for us and love us.

Don't worry. Nate will be getting a story later this year. He was so perfect for Jessica. As we can see, he has flaws that are threatening his peace. He has anger issues, especially when he feels he's been wronged. He's wise beyond his years though, a lot like Noah. If you are a reader of my catalog, you are well aware of who Noah is.

FROM THE AUTHOR...

Decklan... bless his heart. LOL! He knew he messed up, and he was trying his hardest to get Jessica back. His efforts were only pushing her further away. I was glad that they finally had the in-depth talk. It was so needed. Once Jessica realized her flaws, she was able to make things right between them and finalize their breakup. He may even get a story as well.

That damn Storm was Storm. We knew what to expect from that fool and his children. The Hendersons are nowhere near done. You can definitely expect stories from Decaurey and Tyeis, Jakari, and more of the second generation Hendersons.

I truly hope that you enjoyed this drama-filled ride that probably had your feelings all over the place. As always, I gave it my all. Whether you liked it or not, please take the time to leave a review on Amazon and/or Goodreads and wherever else this book is sold.

There's also an amazing playlist on Apple Music and Spotify for this book, under the same title that includes some great R&B tracks to tickle your fancy.

Please keep up with me on Facebook, Instagram, and TikTok (@authormonicawalters), Twitter (@monlwalters), and Clubhouse (@monicawalters). You can also visit my Amazon author page at www.amazon.com/author/monica.walters to view my releases.

Please subscribe to my webpage for updates and sneak peeks of upcoming releases! https://authormonicawalters.com.

For live discussions, giveaways, and inside information on upcoming releases, join my Facebook group, Monica's Romantic Sweet Spot at https://bit.ly/2P2lo6X.

OTHER TITLES BY MONICA WALTERS

Standalones

Love Like a Nightmare

Forbidden Fruit (An Erotic Novella)

Say He's the One

Only If You Let Me (a spin-off of Say He's the One)

On My Way to You (An Urban Romance)

Any and Everything for Love

Savage Heart (A KeyWalt Crossover Novel with Shawty You for Me by T. Key)

I'm In Love with a Savage (A KeyWalt Crossover Novel with Trade It All by T. Key)

Don't Tell Me No (An Erotic Novella)

To Say, I Love You: A Short Story Anthology with the Authors of BLP

Drive Me to Ecstasy

Whatever It Takes: An Erotic Novella

When You Touch Me

When's the Last Time?

Best You Ever Had

Deep As It Goes (A KeyWalt Crossover Novel with Perfect Timing by T. Key)

The Shorts: A BLP Anthology with the Authors of BLP (Made to Love You- Collab with Kay Shanee)

All I Need is You (A KeyWalt Crossover Novel with Divine Love by T. Key)

This Love Hit Different (A KeyWalt Crossover Novel with Something New by T. Key)

Until I Met You

Marry Me Twice

Last First Kiss (a spin-off of Marry Me Twice)

Nobody Else Gon' Get My Love (A KeyWalt Crossover Novel with Better Than Before by T. Key)

Love Long Overdue (A KeyWalt Crossover Novel with Distant Lover by T. Key)

Next Lifetime

Fall Knee-Deep In It

Unwrapping Your Love: The Gift

Who Can I Run To

You're Always on My Mind (a spin-off of Who Can I Run To)

Stuck On You

Full Figured 18 with Treasure Hernandez (Love Won't Let Me Wait)

You Make Me Feel (a spin-off of Stuck On You) (coming soon!)

The Sweet Series
Bitter Sweet

Sweet and Sour

Sweeter Than Before

Sweet Revenge

Sweet Surrender

Sweet Temptation

Sweet Misery

Sweet Exhale

Never Enough (A Sweet Series Update)

Sweet Series: Next Generation
Can't Run From Love

Access Denied: Luxury Love

Still: Your Best

Sweet Series: Kai's Reemergence
Beautiful Mistake

Favorite Mistake

Motives and Betrayal Series
Ulterior Motives

Ultimate Betrayal

Ultimatum: #lovemeorleaveme, Part 1

Ultimatum: #lovemeorleaveme, Part 2

Written Between the Pages Series
The Devil Goes to Church Too

The Book of Noah (A KeyWalt Crossover Novel with The Flow of Jah's Heart by T. Key)

The Revelations of Ryan, Jr. (A KeyWalt Crossover Novel with All That Jazz by T. Key)

The Rebirth of Noah

Behind Closed Doors Series
Be Careful What You Wish For

You Just Might Get It

Show Me You Still Want It

The Country Hood Love Stories
8 Seconds to Love

Breaking Barriers to Your Heart

Training My Heart to Love You

The Country Hood Love Stories: The Hendersons

Blindsided by Love

Ignite My Soul

Come and Get Me

In Way Too Deep

You Belong to Me

Found Love in a Rider

Damaged Intentions: The Soul of a Thug

Let Me Ride

Better the Second Time Around

I Wish I Could Be The One

I Wish I Could Be The One 2

Put That on Everything: A Henderson Family Novella

What's It Gonna Be?

Someone Like You (2nd Generation story)

A Country Hood Christmas with the Hendersons

The Berotte Family Series

Love On Replay

Deeper Than Love

Something You Won't Forget

I'm The Remedy

Love Me Senseless

I Want You Here

Don't Fight The Feeling

When You Dance

I'm All In

Give Me Permission

Force of Nature

Say You Love Me

Where You Should Be

Hard To Love

Made in the USA
Coppell, TX
20 February 2025